Raves For

"..."
—*Chicago Sun-Times*

"Block grabs you...and never lets go."
—*Elmore Leonard*

"[The] one writer of mystery and detective fiction who comes close to replacing the irreplaceable John D. MacDonald."
—*Stephen King*

"The suspense mounts and mounts and mounts...very superior."
—*James M. Cain*

"The narrative is layered with detail, the action is handled with Block's distinctive clarity of style and the ending is a stunning tour de force."
—*The New York Times*

"Lawrence Block is a master of entertainment."
—*Washington Post Book World*

"One of the very best writers now working the beat."
—*The Wall Street Journal*

"Wonderful."
—*USA Today*

"Stellar...a master storyteller in top form."
—*Publishers Weekly*

"Brilliant...For clean, close-to-the-bone prose, the line goes from Dashiell Hammett to James M. Cain to Lawrence Block. He's *that* good."
—*Martin Cruz Smith*

"No one writes the hard-boiled thriller better than Lawrence Block."
—*The San Diego Union*

"Lawrence Block is a master of crime fiction."
—*Jonathan Kellerman*

"Ratchets up the suspense with breathtaking results as only a skilled, inventive and talented writer can do."
—*Orlando Sentinel*

"Lawrence Block is addictive. Make room on your bookshelf."
—*David Morrell*

"Block is awfully good."
—*Los Angeles Times*

"Lawrence Block is America's absolute Number One writer of mystery fiction."
—*Philip Friedman*

"Lawrence Block is finally getting the attention he deserved."
—*Chicago Tribune*

Garrison's eyes opened. He grinned. He was an American businessman on vacation, a real estate speculator who occasionally took a taxi to look at a piece of property. He stayed in a top hotel, ate at good restaurants, tipped a shade too heavily, drank a little too much, and didn't speak a damned word of Spanish. Hardly an assassin, or a secret agent, or anything of the sort. They searched his room, of course, but this happened regularly in every Latin American country. It was a matter of form. Actually, it tended to reassure him, since they searched so clumsily that he knew they were not afraid of him. Otherwise they would take pains to be more subtle.

He stood up, naked and hard-muscled, and walked to his window. He'd been careful to get a room with a window facing on the square. The square was La Plaza de la Republica, a small park surrounding the Palace of Justice. Parades with Fidel at their head made their way up a broad avenue to that plaza. Then Fidel would speak, orating wildly and magnificently from the steps of the palace. From his window Garrison could see those steps.

With the rifle properly mounted on the window ledge, he could place a bullet in Fidel's open mouth...

Killing
CASTRO

by **Lawrence Block**

A HARD CASE CRIME NOVEL

A HARD CASE CRIME BOOK
(HCC-051)
January 2009

Published by

Dorchester Publishing Co., Inc.
200 Madison Avenue
New York, NY 10016

in collaboration with Winterfall LLC

ISBN 0-8439-6113-9
ISBN-13 978-0-8439-6113-3

Cover design by Cooley Design Lab

Typeset by Swordsmith Productions

The name "Hard Case Crime" and the Hard Case Crime logo
are trademarks of Winterfall LLC. Hard Case Crime books are
selected and edited by Charles Ardai.

Printed in the United States of America

Visit us on the web at www.HardCaseCrime.com

KILLING CASTRO

one

The taxi, one headlight out and one fender crimped, cut through downtown Tampa and headed into Ybor City. Turner sat in the back seat with his eyes half closed. He was a tall, thin ramrod of a man who was never tense and yet never entirely relaxed. His hair was the color of damp sand, his eyes steel gray. His lips were thin and he rarely smiled. He was not smiling now.

The stub of a cigarette burned between the second and third fingers of his right hand. The fingers were yellow-brown from the thousands and thousands of cigarettes which had curled their tar-laden smoke around them. He looked at the cigarette, raised it to his lips for a final drag. The smoke was strong. He rolled down the window and flipped the butt into the street.

Night. The street lights were on in Ybor City, Tampa's Latin quarter. Taverns winked seductively in red and green neon. Cubans, Puerto Ricans and Negroes walked the streets, congregated around pool halls and small bars. Here and there butt-twitching hustlers were rushing the season, looking to catch an early trick before the competition got stiff. Turner watched all this through the taxi window, his thin lips not smiling, not frowning. He had bigger things on his mind than corner loungers or early-bird whores.

He was thirty-four years old, and he was wanted for murder.

Thirty-four years old, a man who had done everything and nothing, a man who had been almost everywhere but a man who had never put down roots anywhere. His jobs were a man's jobs—long-haul trucking, where you pushed a heavy load all night long and poured the coffee down your throat to keep your eyes open. Construction work, heavy girders and beams, a pneumatic hammer that churned up the concrete and set your whole body shaking. Merchant seaman hitches, signing on in one port as a deckhand, crawling to another port, maybe making the return trip if you weren't too drunk to find your ship again.

He was thirty-four years old, with no home, no ties. He had been born in Savannah but his father went chasing a better job and they moved north to Philly. Then his father went chasing a better woman and he and his mother were left alone. They kept moving, never staying anywhere too long, never getting attached to a person or a place. It was a pattern he knew well by now. When his mother found a man to marry it wasn't hard for him to move along on his own, find another town, hunt up a job.

Trucking, shipping, wrecking, construction. Drinking hard, loving hard, earning decent dough and spending it as fast as it came in. Savings banks were for married men.

The murder had happened in Charleston. It had happened two months ago, over a girl, and he had been drunk at the time. He closed his eyes and let the scene flash through his memory...

Home again, home from two weeks on a freighter coming up from Galveston, home and off the boat and stopping in a bar for a few quick ones, raw liquor going down fast and hard on an empty stomach. Then the phone, and dialing the girl's number, and no answer. So a few more, a handful of shots chased down the hatch by a handful of beers. And then back home, back to the north side railroad flat to wait for the girl. His key in the lock, turning, the door opening silently.

And then the scene. The girl, his girl, the one who was supposed to be waiting for him, lying flat on her back with her thighs apart and her hips pumping like primed pistons. And the man, fat and swart, between those thighs.

Then madness. He had killed them both, had left them lying nude and dead and bloody. He used the knife he always carried, the small and beautiful knife with the Solingen steel blade. It wasn't a switchblade but if you knew what you were doing you could flip it open quickly, with one hand. He kept it sharp, kept it well oiled. And he had flipped it neatly, expertly.

Then he had cut their throats...

He dug the pack of cigarettes from the pocket of

his flannel shirt, popped one between his lips and scratched a match to light it. He sucked smoke in, shook the match out. A thin jet of smoke trailed out from between his thin lips.

"Much further?"

The cabbie was a Cuban. He said no, it wasn't much further. Turner nodded to himself and sat back in his seat…

Double murder. He hadn't even attempted to disguise it, had closed the bloody knife, dropped it in his pocket, and had gone off to get drunk. He got very drunk. He spent two days drinking, and he woke up on the edge of a marsh south of Charleston. His shoes were gone and his wallet was gone and his watch was gone. The little knife, strangely enough, was still in his pocket.

He ran south. He went through Georgia and Florida, and he wondered how far they were from catching him. They had an old photo of him that they printed in the newspapers, had his fingerprints on file, and it was only a matter of time before they caught him. Sooner or later they would get him. Then they would take him back, put him in jail, try him, convict him, hang him. Justice came quickly in South Carolina.

So he had to get out of the country. If he stayed in the States he was a goner—at thirty-four. That was too young to die. He had to get out of the country, had to get down to South America. You could do that, if you had the money. You could buy new citizenship, set yourself up in business, carve out a neat little niche for yourself. But it took money.

He grinned. It was a brief grin, an almost imperceptible upward curving of the thin lips. It was gone almost instantly.

They were going to give him the money. They were going to give him twenty thousand beautiful dollars—twenty thousand goddamn beautiful dollars. Enough to get him out of the States, enough to put him in Brazil, to buy him Brazilian citizenship, to set him up neatly and permanently. Twenty thousand beautiful goddamn dollars and they were going to hand it to him.

The cab pulled to a halt and the Cuban driver turned to look at Turner. The Cuban smiled easily. "We are here, mister."

Turner nodded. The meter read a dollar and a half. He gave the cabbie two dollars and told him to keep the change. The driver smiled again, showing bad yellow teeth. He asked Turner if he wanted to find a girl, a pretty girl. Turner stepped up onto the sidewalk and told the cabbie to get lost. He waited until the cab pulled away, then walked into the restaurant.

It wasn't much of a place. It had a sign in front supplied by Coca-Cola. It had cracked linoleum on the floor and an ancient Puerto Rican hag behind the counter. The windows looked as though they had never been washed. The clock said it was twenty minutes to nine. Turner was early. He took a stool at the far end of the counter and turned so he could watch the entrance out of the corner of his eye. He ordered black coffee and a plate of rolls. The waitress brought him a basket of sesame seed rolls and a cup of coffee. It was hot, bitter and strong. He ate two of the rolls and drank some of the coffee.

Twenty thousand dollars and they were giving it to him.

He lit another cigarette. It wasn't that simple, he thought. First he had to commit a murder. One murder to make up for the other murders, one planned killing to get him out of the jam that a double unplanned killing had placed him in. Only there was a difference, because that double murder had involved people who didn't matter. A cheap waterfront slut and a fat, dark dock-walloper. No one important.

This planned murder, this twenty-grand homicide, this was different. He wasn't going to knock off just anyone.

He was going to murder Fidel Castro.

Hiraldo came into the restaurant at four minutes to nine. Turner saw him out of the corner of his eye but did not turn around. He picked up another roll and took a bite of it, then washed it down with more coffee. He was working on his second cup.

He waited while Hiraldo made his way to the back of the restaurant and took the stool beside him. Hiraldo was a short man, fat-bellied, mostly bald. He smiled easily, showing a great many gold fillings. He looked soft and foolish. Turner knew better.

"You have been waiting long?"

"Not long," Turner said.

"The others have arrived. They are in the apartment of a friend, a sympathizer. We will join them."

"You're calling the shots."

"Finish your coffee," Hiraldo said. "There is no hurry."

Turner ate another roll and finished his coffee. He put money on the counter. He got up and let the fat little Cuban lead him out of the restaurant. Hiraldo's car, a three-year-old Chevrolet, was parked around the corner. They went to it. Hiraldo drove. He took several turns, and Turner decided that he did this to keep him from knowing where they were. It didn't work. Turner knew exactly where they were. He sat with his hand in his pocket, his fingers closed around the little knife with the Solingen steel blade.

Hiraldo said: "This is very important, Señor Turner. This lunatic Castro is a bad smell in the noses of all Cubans. You will be performing a service."

Turner said nothing.

"You will be ridding Cuba of a menace, a despotic maniac. You will be striking a blow at the Communist world conspiracy. You will be—"

"Forget it," Turner said.

The Cuban looked at him, smiled and showed his gold teeth. "I do not understand," he said.

"The patriotic bit. Forget it."

"You are not a patriot?"

"I'm not a patriot. I'm not a hero. I tried that once—they called it Korea and it was mud and Chinamen screaming and people dying. Men dying. Ever see a man die, Hiraldo?"

"Yes."

"Yeah. To hell with it. I don't want to be a hero. You got a flag to wave, you can wave it at somebody else. It was Machado, then it was Batista, now it's Castro. Every time anybody turns around you guys got another fat cat sitting on the top of the heap. They all stink."

"Our country has problems."

"Yeah. Problems. I got problems of my own. You understand my problems, Hiraldo?"

"Money?"

"Money," Turner said. "Twenty thousand dollars. For twenty grand I'm your boy, you're my boss, that's all. I don't care if I'm killing Castro or Batista. You understand?"

Hiraldo moistened his lips. "I understand."

"Good," Turner said.

They lapsed into silence. The Cuban parked the car in front of a small red-brick building which had seen better days. The brick was in need of repair and many of the windows were broken. Turner saw light around the edges of dark burlap curtains in a fourth-floor window. No other lights were on. They got out of the

car and walked up an unlighted stairway to the fourth
floor. Hiraldo knocked twice, paused, knocked three
times, paused, knocked twice.

Oh, Christ, Turner thought. *They've got signals.
Straight out of a spy movie. The stupid bastards have
got signals!*

The door opened inward. They went inside, first
Hiraldo, then Turner. There were six of them waiting.
A thin Cuban with a pencil-line mustache leaned indo-
lently against a far wall picking his teeth with a match-
stick. His eyes were lazy. Another Cuban sat in an easy
chair with his legs crossed at the knees. He was an
older man, older than Hiraldo—in his fifties or maybe
in his sixties. It was hard for Turner to tell.

There were four Americans. Turner glanced quickly
at each of them, sized them up, then ignored them.
A young kid, he couldn't be more than twenty-three,
probably closer to eighteen. Young, green, hardly old
enough to shave. Skinny, too. Dark hair, a full mouth, a
white sport shirt open at the neck. He sat in a bridge
chair and didn't look around.

Another, closer to Turner's age, with a broad forehead and stevedore arms. Brawn, Turner thought.
Muscle. Not much for thinking but hell in a back alley
scramble. And that was fine, because it never hurt you
to have a little muscle on your team.

A third, and this one looked like a goddamn accoun-
tant. Wire-rimmed glasses, a face as determinedly

Anglo-Saxon as Yorkshire pudding. Wearing a pin-
stripe suit, yet, with a regimental-striped tie. What was
he doing there?

The fourth. Turner studied him, then went over
and sat next to him on the old sofa. This one, Turner
thought, was the only one who counted. Maybe thirty-
five, maybe forty-five, somewhere in the middle and it
didn't much matter. This one, this last one, was the
one who would be running things. The others were
jumping out of their skins but this one, with a strong
chin and sharp eyes and wiry muscles, he was calm.
Well, fine, Turner thought. *This boy can take charge. I
thought I was going to have to run things myself. But
let him have the headaches.*

Hiraldo took out a pack of Cuban cigarettes and
began offering them around. The thin man with the
glasses took one, accepted a light. The others passed
them up. Hiraldo lit a cigarette of his own, shuffled
around for a moment, then started to speak.

Introductions came first. Turner listened, learned
everybody's name. The young kid was Jim Hines, the
muscle man was Matt Garth, the thin one with glasses
was Earl Fenton, the take-charge type was Ray Garrison. Turner was introduced as Michael Turner. *Mike
for short,* he thought. *Except for a girl in Charleston,
who used to call him Mickey. But that was before he
cut her throat...*

°

Fenton drew on the Cuban cigarette, inhaled the strong smoke. He almost coughed but he managed to control it, to blow out the smoke slowly and take a breath of air to clear his lungs. As much as they could be cleared, anyway, he thought. Smoking was a hell of a habit. Bad for you. Maybe if he had never started smoking—

He looked at Hiraldo. It was strange the way the man could not speak without moving his hands, without pacing the floor. Fenton dragged on the cigarette again and this time he did not choke on the tobacco smoke. He listened to the Cuban.

"Five men with a mission," Hiraldo was saying. "Five men, five small men, but together you can tumble a colossus. This lunatic, this Fidel, he has set himself up as lord and master of the Cuban nation. He has betrayed a most vital revolution, has climbed upon Señor Batista's throne and has stepped into Señor Batista's bloody shoes. He has—"

Fenton stopped listening. A long-winded little man, he decided. One would think men of action had little time for speech-making. But evidently this Mr. Hiraldo was long on words and short on action.

Action! That was the point of it all, was it not? It had to be, Fenton thought. There came a time when it was no longer enough to vote, no longer enough to work from nine to five in the Metropolitan Bank of Lynbrook, no longer enough to come home, to eat a solitary meal, to watch a program on a television set, to go down to the corner tavern for a glass of beer and an hour or two of easy conversation. There came a time when time itself was ebbing, when the world was running away from you. When you had to act, and act fast, because there was little time.

So little time.

"I believe you are all acquainted with the terms," Hiraldo said.

"Twenty grand," Turner said shortly. Fenton looked at him, saw strength coupled with desperation. What was it that Thoreau had written? Most men lead lives of quiet desperation, something like that. A wealth of meaning in a few simple words.

"Twenty thousand dollars," Hiraldo said. "For each of you. A total, in short, of one hundred thousand dollars, money put up by those men who love Cuba and wish to see her liberated. One hundred thousand dollars, a fit price for the head of Fidel Castro."

"How do we get it?" It was that Matt Garth talking, the heavyset, muscular one. Fenton looked at him.

Hiraldo said: "It will be held for you."

"And suppose you welsh?"

Hiraldo didn't understand. Turner explained that Garth wanted a guarantee of payment.

"Like half in advance, half later," Garth said.

Hiraldo would not go along with that. He explained another system, something involving the deposit of the funds in a bank account in some manner which would be a guarantee of good faith all around. Fenton did not bother listening to the explanation. The money hardly mattered. The money was unimportant, irrelevant, immaterial. Money was good only for what it would buy. The money would buy very little for Fenton. What he wanted had no price tag, was carried on the shelves of no department store.

No, the money was unimportant. Of course one could not help but wonder where it was coming from. A band of impoverished Cuban refugees would hardly be able to scrape together a round sum of one hundred thousand dollars. Who was financing the assassination? Tobacco and sugar planters? Oil refiners? Batista fascists hungry to regain power? Americans unwilling to tolerate a Communist nation ninety miles offshore?

Interesting questions, Fenton thought. Fascinating questions. But, like the money itself, irrelevant and immaterial as far as he himself was concerned. Just as irrelevant and immaterial as the money.

What mattered was the action, the purpose. No matter who his opponents and what their motives, this man called Fidel Castro was an evil force in the overall scheme of things, a dictator who had to be destroyed. And he, Earl Fenton, would be a contributor to his destruction. That mattered, that was important. That and little else.

Fenton lit another cigarette from the first. This new cigarette had a filter tip, and Fenton looked at it for a moment before putting it back in his mouth. Bad form, chain-smoking. Bad for your health. Even if they were filtered, cigarettes could hurt you. He sucked smoke into his lungs, winced, hoped no one had noticed the wince. So little time…

So little time to act, to exist. To kill, of course. He had time for that. Time to kill—that was what it was, what it all boiled down to, and the unintentional word play summed it all up. Time to kill.

Time to kill Castro. Because the man was rotten, the man deserved to die. All Fenton knew was what he read in the papers. Castro executed, and Castro dictated, and Castro was a despot, and Castro was probably power mad, and Castro had to die. That was all.

"You will divide now," Hiraldo was saying. "Two and two and one. You—Turner—will go with Hines. Fenton, you will go with Garth. You, Garrison, will—"

"Hold on, Hiraldo."

"Mr. Garrison?"

Garrison took a breath, let it out in a long sigh. Fenton watched him, saw the assurance of the man, the lazy strength. "If you want somebody to follow your stage directions," he said, "find another boy."

"How do you mean?"

"You know damn well what I mean," Garrison said. "If I play this game, I play it my way. I don't follow somebody else's plan. We—the five of us—do the shooting, the killing, the dirty work. We'll write our own script."

"And you think I wish to plan this assassination? This removal of a tyrant?"

"I don't know what you wish," Garrison told him. "I don't care what you want. All I know is what *I* want, and that is to go to Cuba, get Castro, then come back here and pick up twenty grand. That's all. And I want to do it my way."

Hiraldo seemed partially amused, partly irritated. Fenton watched the play of emotions over his face. "Let me explain my position," the short Cuban said.

"I'm listening," Garrison told him.

Hiraldo said: "Believe me, I have no intention of... uh...drawing the plans for the assassination. I am not an assassin."

"Congratulations."

Hiraldo ignored the interruption. "As you may know," he said, "it will be somewhat difficult for you five to enter Cuba. You cannot go in a body. You cannot take a boat or fly in a commercial plane. You cannot—"

"We can't walk on water," Garrison snapped. "Get to the point."

Hiraldo's tone was icy. "I am planning a landing," he said. "A landing of five men. Two, and two, and one."

"Go on."

"Turner and Hines will go to a house in Miami. They will be expected. They will be escorted to a boat, a fast private ship which will put them ashore on the northern coast of Cuba. They will be met by sympathizers and introduced into the city of Havana."

Garrison said nothing.

"Fenton and Garth will go to another house," Hiraldo continued. "A house here in Tampa, in Ybor City. They will soon be taken to a private airstrip off the Tamiami Trail. A plane will be waiting there. It will take them to Oriente Province, to the hills where rebels, at this very moment, are fighting the butcher who—"

"Skip the speeches, Hiraldo."

The Cuban sighed. "They will meet these freedom fighters who will help them in any way they can. And you, Mr. Garrison—"

"—will get to Cuba under my own power," the man said. "And I'll do as I damn please, and will play it whatever way I want. I don't need your boats or your planes or your sympathizers or your freedom fighters. I don't want a goddamned soul to know where I am or what I'm doing. You got that straight, Hiraldo?"

"I have it straight."

"Fine," Ray Garrison said. "I'm glad we understand each other. I'm going to Cuba. When your boy Castro is dead, I'll be back. Have the money waiting for me."

He stood up, his big body uncoiling easily. For the first time he seemed to be aware of Fenton, of Turner, Hines and Garth. "You boys take it easy," he said. "Don't let this spic hand you a hard time. I'll see you all in Cuba."

And Fenton watched Ray Garrison walk out of the room.

After that it was simpler, quieter, easier. After that, Fenton could sit at ease, smoke one cigarette after the other and think his own thoughts while Hiraldo talked of trivia. He, Fenton, was supposed to go with Garth, to live in a house in Ybor City and take a plane to the Oriente hills. And from there, somehow, they were supposed to kill Castro. It seemed improbable, at best.

But he would see what happened. He lit a cigarette from a butt, ground the butt under his heel. Hiraldo talked too much, as Garrison had said. Hiraldo dealt in words, not deeds, and wordy men were what Fenton was trying to escape.

So little time…

He remembered the beginning. The beginning of awareness, at any rate, if not the beginning of it all. How could you pin down beginnings?

Maybe the beginning was long ago. Maybe it all started with birth, many years ago, in Lynbrook. A nice town, Lynbrook. Quiet, peaceful and typically New England. He had been born there and he had lived there, had gone to school, then moved on to the bank. His life was a mirror of the town—quiet, peaceful and typically New England. No wife, because there had never been a woman with whom he'd fallen in love. No mistress; a bank teller in a tiny town cannot afford an affair. Just the job, a few friends, a glass of beer and a book in the evenings, a cup of coffee and the morning paper at dawn. Was that the beginning?

No, he thought. That was the foundation, perhaps.

The groundwork. That prepared him, made him a man ready to wait a few more years for retirement, a man who had saved money painstakingly for those years of leisure, the good years, the lazy, self-indulging years a man like himself looked forward to.

Then it began.

It had begun with a pain—a small pain in the chest that came often enough to send him to his doctor. Maybe a heart condition, maybe he would have to start taking it easier.

But it turned out to be something worse—something frightening, inevitable and inexorable. It was a little six-letter word which translated itself into a smaller, colder five-letter word.

The six-letter word was cancer.

The five-letter word was death.

Carcinoma of the lung—lung cancer. How much time, Doctor? More than a month and less than a year. You can have an operation, you can have radium treatments, you can have X-rays. Yes, and we can apply leeches, we can let blood, we can give you hot baths and cold baths and dose you with vitamins and fill you full of antibiotics. And whatever we do, Earl Fenton, in more than a month and less than a year we will bury you. You will be dead and we will place you into a hole and fill that hole with earth.

More than a month, less than a year.

So very little time...

*

The very thin Cuban with the pencil-line mustache drove Turner and Hines from Tampa to Miami. It was neither a short nor a long drive. The car was a last year's Cadillac and the thin Cuban drove it as though driver and car were component parts of a single mechanism. The Cuban did not stop once, not for gas, not for coffee, not to pass water. He stopped at last in front of a concrete-block-and-stucco house in what seemed to be a suburb of Miami. Hines wasn't sure where they were. He had never been to Miami before, had in fact never been south of Baltimore before. He got out of the car along with the Cuban and Turner.

The Cuban led them to the door. False dawn was streaking the sky. Hines looked at the watch on his wrist, saw that it was almost five in the morning. They had been up the whole night, then. When was the last time he'd been up that long? At school, of course. At Cornell, cramming for exams, working like a Turk for finals.

It seemed like a million years ago. Christ, he was a college kid, he was supposed to be at school studying for tests and going to proms and laying coeds in the back seats of cars and otherwise engaging in the hysterical procedure of getting an education. He was a kid, a punk, a wet-behind-the-ears kid all of nineteen years old, a scared little kid with nothing on the ball, and now he was supposed to go into a foreign country and kill a man named Fidel Castro.

Who the hell *was* he? A college kid. A kid whose

father had sold insurance and whose mother lived on it now, an upstate-New-York-appleknocker kind of kid, a kid who'd never had a gun in his hand in his life. Kids in Utica didn't play with guns. The town was a cultural backwater; teenage gangs weren't the rage, and you could grow up slowly and leisurely, accepting middle-class values because that was simply the way things were, hoping to grow up and marry a girl right off the *Saturday Evening Post*'s prettiest cover, raise a few children and make a comfortable living.

So Utica was bad training ground for an assassin. And so was Cornell, for God's sake. Jesus, Castro was some damned kind of a folding bed, not a man you were going to kill.

When you stopped to think about it, it was kind of nuts.

Nuts, ridiculous, crazy, wet-brained. It didn't make any sense at all. There were four others, and one of them was a brainless hunk of muscle and another was a rugged outdoor type and another was a little old guy who reminded Hines of his father who had died several years ago of coronary thrombosis and who had peddled insurance in Utica. And the fourth one, this Turner character next to him, the strong silent type who was made out of wrought iron. A hell of an odd bunch, a crazy bunch, and the bunch was made much crazier by the addition of one, James Hines.

Nuts.

The Cuban had unlocked the door, had given them

the key, had left them. Turner was in the kitchen making coffee. Hines sat down in the living room. He couldn't sit still, had to get up and pace the floor. He went on pacing until Turner came back with two mugs of coffee.

"It's instant," Turner said. "And I couldn't find milk or sugar. Black all right with you?"

"It's fine."

"Then take a cup and drink it. And sit down, for God's sake. You make me nervous."

He took the coffee, sat down, sipped it and burned his mouth. Turner was drinking the coffee as if it were room temperature.

"How can you drink it so hot?"

"I was a trucker for a while," Turner said. "Long-distance hauling. When you stop on the road you want to get coffee down fast. You can't wait for it to cool. It's something you get used to."

Hines nodded. Well, you ask and you find out. He waited for his coffee to cool a little, then sipped it.

Turner lit a cigarette. He stood up, sat down.

Turner said: "Drink more coffee, wait an hour. Then get the hell out of here and catch the first plane north."

"What do you mean?"

"I mean you're a kid," Turner snapped. "A young idealistic kid in the wrong boat. You can get out while you've got a chance and go home to Mom and Dad."

"Dad's dead."

"I'm sorry."

"The hell you're sorry," Hines said. "Forget it. You were saying something and you might as well finish it."

The tone surprised both of them. Then Turner said: "You don't know what it's all about. You think this Castro is a dictator, so we'll be heroes and kill him. You're the only hero in the crowd, kid. I'm not here to play hero. I want twenty grand. I *need* twenty grand. I killed a man and a woman and if I stay in this country they'll hang me for it. They'll take me to Charleston and hang me."

Hines thought, *This man is a murderer. He's telling me all this. I'm supposed to be shocked or something.* But he wasn't shocked. He thought only that now he knew Turner's reason, now he knew why Turner was in on the deal. It was an answer and nothing more.

"And Garth," Turner said. "The one with muscles instead of brains. You think he's a goddamn freedom fighter?"

"I think he's a slob."

"Yeah," Turner said. "A slob. You tell him to hit and he hits. No brain, no ideals, nothing. A slob. How about Garrison?"

"He's a bounty hunter."

Turner was nodding emphatically, smoke from his cigarette trailing out between his thin lips. "You got it," he said. "A bounty hunter. There's a price on Castro and he wants to collect it. It's a business with him. He'd kill anybody, anywhere, any time, for the right price. He'd kill you for twenty grand—or me. Or his mother."

"And Fenton?"

"Skip him," Turner said. "I didn't figure him yet. Let's go on. How about Hiraldo?"

"He's a hired hand," Hines said. "You noticed Hiraldo. You didn't notice the old guy, did you?"

"I noticed him."

Hines said: "You know who he is?" Turner shook his head. "His name is Juan Carboa," Hines said. "He's a businessman. He has a cute business. He finances revolutions."

"I didn't know that."

"He's been around for years," Hines said, ready to talk now, surer of himself. "There was a man in Cuba named Machado. Carboa collected money, armed a sergeant named Batista. Batista threw out Machado."

"You learn all this in school?"

"Just listen to me," Hines said. "I'm proving something. About idealists."

"Keep talking."

"Then Carboa raised more money," Hines said. "Later, years later, he financed somebody named Castro, a law student with a beard—Fidel Castro. And Castro threw out Batista. Now Juan Carboa is financing somebody who's going to throw out Castro. Each time he does this, one hell of a lot of money winds up in Juan Carboa's hands. He's making a living out of revolutions."

Turner made no comment.

"I know a lot," Hines said. "About idealism."

"So what's your angle?"

Hines shrugged. Maybe you could talk too much, he thought. Maybe there was a point at which you should shut up. Maybe when you opened your wounds you were just asking somebody to pour salt in them.

"Come on," Turner said. "Everybody's got an angle. What's yours?"

"I'm not an idealist," Hines said.

"No?"

"No. I had a brother, Turner. An older brother, six years older than I am. He was an idealist, Turner."

"Yeah?"

"Just shut up and listen. He was an idealist, a great guy. I loved the bastard. You got that? He taught me things, spent a lot of time with me. It was the older brother-younger brother bit and I loved him for it. So Castro went up against Batista and Joe—my brother—went to the hills to help out. He didn't come in on the tail end. He was there almost from the beginning, before half the people in this country ever heard of Castro. He was there. He fought and he starved and he was there when they won. You got that?"

Turner looked at him.

"So this brother of mine was there, and they won when everybody expected them to lose. They were just a band of kids with beards fighting a professional army and, damn it, they won. And Castro was on top."

Turner lit another cigarette. Hines stopped for a minute. This was the hard part, this was where it got tough to keep going. But he had to get it out, it was important now and he had to tell Turner. Somehow, it was important that Turner be told.

"This Castro," he said, "he got on an anti-American kick. And there was Joe, an American, an idealist. He was on Castro's side, but he was still an American."

He paused for breath and then went on. "Castro called it revolutionary justice. He said Joe Hines betrayed the revolution and had to get his. With revolutionary justice you don't need a trial. All you need is a firing squad. They took my brother, put him in front of a firing squad and shot him deader than hell. So I'm going to Cuba, Turner, and I'm going to kill this son-of-a-bitch, Castro, and if that's idealism you can shove it straight up your ass."

Neither of them said anything for a while. Then Turner got up, took the coffee cups, carried them to the kitchen. Hines sat in his chair and looked at his hands. They were not trembling. *I'm steady as a goddamn rock*, he thought. *No shakes or nothing. Just steady. Gibraltar.*

Turner came back, handed him a cup of coffee. They drank in silence. When they set down empty cups Turner offered him a cigarette. He shook his head and Turner lit one for himself.

"What I said before," Turner apologized, "about you grabbing a plane and going home. Just forget I said it, okay?"

"Sure."

"How old are you, Hines?"

"Nineteen. Why?"

"No reason. You ever have a woman?"

Hines looked at his hands. He took a deep breath.

"Well? Did you?"

"No."

"Don't be ashamed of it, for Christ's sake. Look, it's late, we're both tired. There are bedrooms in the back. We'll sack out for eight hours, then send out for some food and some liquor. You drink?"

"Sure."

"Good," Turner said. "We'll get some food and we'll get some liquor, and I'll call somebody on the phone and get a couple of girls. We'll eat the food and we'll drink the liquor and we'll lay the girls. Then we'll go to Cuba and get our asses shot off. That sound okay to you?"

"Sure," Hines said.

"Fine," Turner said. "Now let's get some sleep."

two

Fidel Castro was born on the thirteenth of August in 1926. His father was a Spaniard, a Galician who settled in Oriente Province and became rich from sugar and lumber. Fidel grew up on his father's farm at Biran, in the municipality of Mayari on the north coast of Oriente, near Nipe Bay. He ran barefoot in his father's fields, hauled lumber with a tractor. He was baptized as a Roman Catholic and went to church schools in Santiago.

Fidel Castro was seven years old when Batista took over the island. Fulgencio Batista, a tough-minded sergeant in the Cuban Army, managed to rally the armed forces around him and grab power in the turmoil surrounding the revolt which ousted Machado. The young Fidel Castro grew to maturity in Batista's Cuba, an island where personal liberty was ground out beneath the iron heel of dictatorship.

He attended the Christian Brothers' Colegio La Salle, then transferred to complete his grade school education at the Jesuit Colegio Dolores. He played a bugle in the school band and wore his first uniform, a navy-blue outfit with a white Sam Browne belt.

In 1942, while the rest of the world abandoned itself to the early years of the second world war, Fidel was sent to high school in Havana at the Colegio Belen. It was there that his talents for leadership came to the foreground. He was outstanding in his studies and in athletics as well, pitching for the baseball team, playing basketball, running for the track squad. By the time he graduated in June of 1945, he had made his choice of a vocation. He was going to become a lawyer.

The University of Havana, where Fidel Castro en-rolled in the fall of that year, was a fundamentally different sort of place from North American universi-ties. Latin American colleges have, throughout history, played a predominant role in the politics of their nations. Revolutions and uprisings are fomented there, radical thought is encouraged. Panty raids and homecoming rallies are unknown in Latin American colleges. Latin American students have weightier concerns to occupy their time.

It was at the university that Fidel's future was molded. He entered the Law School, became embroiled in student affairs. He was an impressive figure—tall, good-looking, with strong features, a quick mind, and a fine speaking voice. In a short time he had become a prominent campus figure, an artist at political manip-ulation.

But in the summer of 1947 Castro's revolutionary zeal interrupted his academic studies. He joined an

*expeditionary force training in the hills of Oriente,
preparing to invade the Dominican Republic to overthrow Trujillo, the island republic's long-term dictator.
There Fidel got his first taste of military life, a taste
which developed with the years.*

*The invasion was premature, and a failure. The
Dominican government got wind of the plans and sent
a note of protest to the Cuban government. The Cuban
president was quick to co-operate with Trujillo. Frigates
of the Cuban navy intercepted the invasion force and
squelched the attempt. Castro himself jumped over-
board with his submachine gun in hand and swam to
shore holding the gun high overhead.*

*Fidel returned to the university once more and
turned his sights on campus politics. He accepted
Communist support in the campaign for election to the
vice-presidency of the Law School's student government, then spun around to unleash a spirited campaign
against the campus Communists. When the president
resigned, Castro stepped to the helm of the student
government.*

*He was learning. He was a natural politician, quick
to sense the twists and turns of the game, ready to
cement allegiances for his own personal gain. He was a
pragmatic idealist—his goals were high and worthy,
but he was willing to use less than idealistic means to
achieve those goals. Fidel went on, continuing with his
studies, advancing himself as a politician. Cuban poli-*

tics were disorganized at the time. Batista had been living abroad in voluntary exile at Daytona Beach, Florida, since 1944; in that year he had finally held an honest election, the first since 1933, and had been beaten badly. But the administration which followed Batista was almost as corrupt, furthering the interests of the Cuban upper classes to the exclusion of the poor. Fidel dreamed of a free Cuba, her land redistributed to the peasants, her citizens equal before the law. In 1948 Fidel married; a year later his first son was born. In 1950 he graduated from the University of Havana and hung out his shingle as a lawyer. His idealism prevailed, and he spent the bulk of his time defending men and women of the lower classes, rarely collecting a fee. The common people of Havana knew Castro. They saw him as a good man, a man with their interests at heart. And how did Castro see himself? As an embryonic politician, a man with a future in Cuba. In those days, living in Havana, defending the poor in the Cuban courts, maybe Fidel Castro did not dream of revolutions. After all, Batista was in exile in Florida. The government was corrupt and reforms were needed desperately, but maybe he figured there was no reform which could not be achieved through legal means.

After all, in the elections of 1952, Fidel Castro intended to run for congress.

But there were no elections in 1952. That was the year Batista, hungry once more for power, returned *from Daytona Beach to Cuba. On March tenth he entered Camp Columbia. His vast fortune had been depleted in a divorce settlement and he intended to rebuild it, squeezing the money from the island of Cuba. He seized control of the army and sent the legitimate government running for their lives.*

Batista's coup was conducted swiftly and efficiently. In no time at all he had complete control of the government. Foreign nations extended diplomatic recognition to him and the Cuban people themselves did not dare to raise their voices against him. But one young lawyer in Havana had different ideas. He saw only that a corrupt dictator once again had his grip on Cuba. He knew that this was wrong, and he tried to do something about it.

Castro submitted a brief to the Cuban courts contesting the Batista government. The brief was thrown out. He wrote a letter to Batista, calling for honest elections and representative government. The letter, of course, was ignored.

Batista remained in power.

And then Fidel Castro realized something. He saw that the Batista dictatorship was not the sort to be ousted through parliamentary means. He saw that the reforms he envisioned, the redistribution of land and the social progress, would not come about gradually. Batista's Cuba was a toy for the rich, run for the benefit of corrupt Cuban politicians.

Batista could not be reformed. He could only be overthrown. He could not be changed but had to be thrown out bodily. The only politics which would work in Cuba were the politics of the knife and the Sten gun, the politics of guerrilla warfare in the hills and underground intrigue in the cities.

The following year, on the 26th of July in 1953, he began.

three

When Garrison walked out on Hiraldo, he went to a bar a block away. The air was warm and close. He walked quickly, eyes front. He knew there was a man behind him but he did not turn around.

The bar was dark and dirty, filled with Cubans. Garrison stood near the rear and nursed a glass of draft beer. He saw his tail come in, a hollow-eyed Cuban wearing horn-rimmed glasses. Now he had a problem. The tail could be one of Hiraldo's men checking up on the would-be assassins. But he could just as easily be somebody else's man. Fidel's, for example.

Garrison thought it over. He finished his beer, left the bar, caught a taxi. His tail followed him out of the bar and stepped into an old Mercury idling at the curb. The Merc pulled out and stayed behind the taxi.

"In case you didn't know," the cabbie said, "you got a tail."

"I know," Garrison said.

"Want to lose him?"

"No," Garrison said. "Pretend you don't know he's there. Find me a cheap, quiet hotel. A dump."

The cabbie found one, an ancient building with a neon sign that said *Hotel* and nothing more. Garrison climbed four crumbling wooden steps, walked into a lobby that smelled of disinfectant and stale beer. A clerk wearing a green eye shade took Garrison's three dollars in advance and gave him a key to a room on the third floor. There was no elevator. Garrison climbed the stairs and let himself into his room, locking the door behind him.

There was an unmade bed, a dresser with cigarette burns around the edges, a cane-bottomed wooden chair. Garrison turned on the light and sat on the edge of the bed. After ten minutes had passed he turned out the light. It was their move, he thought. Let them make it. He figured they'd give him time to get to sleep, then sneak in to do their dirty work. He'd fool them—if his ruse worked—and hand them their heads.

He waited for half an hour—it seemed like an eternity—ears alert for the slightest sound.

They were sloppy. He heard their footsteps on the staircase, heard unintelligible whispering in the hallway. He tiptoed to the door as he heard the scratching of a knife blade prying the door open. Then silence.

The door moved inward. Garrison had his gun in his hand, the sleek Beretta he carried in a special pocket sewn into his jacket. He held the gun by the barrel now. This had to be silent. Even in a cheap fleabag hotel you didn't take chances with gunfire.

There were two of them, two Cubans standing in his room, letting their eyes grow accustomed to the darkness. One—the fellow who had been driving the

Mercury—had a large revolver in his hand. The other held a knife.

The gun first. Garrison was close, close enough to reach out and touch them, close enough to smell their sweat. His body relaxed, shifted into gear, unwound in fluid motion. The Beretta went up and then down. There was a dull thud, a shifting, a grunt. The man with the gun fell, face forward, into the room.

Garrison pushed the door shut and crouched, ready to spring.

Now it was cute. Now they were alone in total darkness, he and the one with the knife, a switchblade stiletto with a four-inch blade.

Garrison had the advantage; he could see better, his eyes were used to the dim light. But the Cuban was smart, refusing to make a move until he could make out Garrison's silhouette. Tense moments idled by before the man lunged like a cobra, the knife coming up in a liquid underhand motion. Garrison dodged, grabbed for the Cuban's arm, missed.

The knife snaked in again. Garrison backed off, bumped into the bed and cursed. The Cuban was ready for another try and Garrison ducked just in time, the knife moving wide over a shoulder. The Cuban was breathing hoarsely, moving in for the kill—he hoped. Garrison got away from the bed, found the cane-bottomed chair, hefted it and threw it. It took the knife artist in the chest and sent him reeling backwards, but he came up quickly, the knife still in his hand.

Time pressed Garrison. The other Cuban, the one on the floor, was coming to. Garrison heard him trying to struggle to his feet and he knew it was now or never. He wished he still had his Beretta, but that was gone, probably under the bed.

The Cuban charged but Garrison was ready. He sidestepped, moved in hard, catching the Cuban with a hand on his wrist and another hand on his upper arm. His own knee came up quickly. With the knee under the Cuban's elbow it was very simple. He broke the man's arm as easily as he would have snapped a twig. The stiletto clattered to the floor. The Cuban moaned like a girl, went to his knees, and Garrison knocked him out with a kick to the temple.

Another kick sent the other Cuban off to sleep again.

He switched on the light and went through their pockets. The knife wielder carried a few bills and a handful of change, nothing more. Garrison took the money. The man with the gun had a wallet containing a Cuban driver's license, a passport, more money. The passport had a recent date.

Castristas, Garrison thought. Fidel's bullyboys. And they had come to kill him. So Castro's men suspected something was cooking. Well, that made it harder. They might know something was cooking but they didn't know what. Garrison shrugged his shoulders—twenty grand was a lot of money, the kind of dough you don't get unless there's danger in the deal.

And this pair wouldn't make trouble. Garrison grinned, found the stiletto. The man who held the gun, the driver, was stirring again. Garrison cut his throat easily, then slit the throat of the other Cuban. He wiped his prints from the knife, the door, the various articles of furniture in the room he might have touched. He found his Beretta, returned it to the pocket where it belonged and left the room, closing the door behind him.

He left the hotel. The maid would find a surprise in the morning. If they had maids in such a dump. And if anything could surprise them.

He laughed, a quick private laugh. Then he caught a cab and rode to the Splendora.

The Splendora was a medium-priced hotel in downtown Tampa where Garrison was registered under the name of David Palmer. He went to his room on the top floor and packed his suitcase. That wasn't difficult— Garrison traveled light. The suitcase, when full, contained one lightweight cord suit, one pair of tennis sneakers, two summer shirts, a few changes of underwear and a few pairs of socks. There was one book, a slim volume of poems by Rimbaud. Garrison did not read much but he happened to like Rimbaud. He carried his suitcase to the lobby, paid his bill and checked out. He left no forwarding address.

His car, an old blue Ford, was parked near the

Splendora. He had bought the car in New Orleans a
week ago as David Palmer and had driven it to Tampa.
Now he put his suitcase in the trunk and locked it.
There was a gun in the trunk, a high-powered rifle
with a scope sight that had cost a little more than the
car. It, too, had been purchased in New Orleans. He
got behind the wheel and drove out of Tampa.

Garrison was thirty-seven. In 1924, while Coolidge
was being re-elected President of the United States, Ray
Garrison was being born in a town about as far from
Tampa as you could go without leaving the country. The
town was Birch Fork, in Washington, a very small town
in the central part of the state. He lived in Birch Fork
for seventeen years. Then he enlisted in the Marine
Corps.

When he thought about it, which happened rarely, it
occurred to him that the history of those seventeen years
in Birch Fork was best told in terms of the weapons he
had owned. He was, first, a solitary child and, next, a
solitary youth. He spent those early years in the woods.
He never went without a weapon.

When he was seven he made a slingshot. The stock
was made of strong wood and the sling was a stout
rubber band. The slingshot was inaccurate at first, but
he worked on it and with it, practicing constantly.
Before long he was able to get squirrels and jack rab-
bits, sometimes a bird or two. He didn't kill the small
game out of blood lust but simply for target practice.
It just wasn't the same when you shot at pop bottles or

tin cans. You needed a living target to make it all real.

When he was eleven his father bought him a BB gun for his birthday. He loved the gun, but it was inexpensive and the barrel was untrue. First he learned to make up for the gun's inaccuracy by aiming a little high and wide. Then one day the gun irritated him. He took it apart, hammered out the slight dent that was ruining the gun's aim, and put it back together again.

Three years later he got a .22. This he bought himself, out of money he had earned at odd jobs and chores, and it was a beautiful gun with a highly polished stock and gleaming metal parts. This was a real gun, not a toy, and he was good with it. A year or two later he added a shotgun to his collection. He hadn't liked shotguns at first—the wide pattern they cast seemed to him to be making things too easy for the hunter—but he quickly learned the subtleties of the shotgun and grew to like it.

He never ate what he killed, never brought it home, never stuffed it, skinned it or mounted it. He was interested in guns, and in the sport. He was not interested in dead bodies.

Then 1941, and Pearl Harbor, and the Marines. He was in all the way, in for the whole Pacific campaign, jumping from one ugly little island to the next, with men dying around him and in front of him. He used an M-1, a BAR and a machine gun. He learned hand-to-hand combat. He lived in death's presence, and looked it squarely in the face. He thought often of death, wondered about it, hoped he would avoid it. He went through the war without a wound, without a scratch.

And the war was over. The Marines knocked off Guadalcanal, and Tarawa, Iwo and the rest and then some bastard of a flyboy pushed a lever and stole the show. A bomb hit Hiroshima, and a few days later another one hit Nagasaki, and then the war was over and he came back to the States again.

When he got back to Birch Fork his home was gone. His mother and father were dead, and there was no reason to stick around. One day he went into the woods with his rifle and took a shot at a squirrel or two, but the thrill was gone. When you were used to hunting men you didn't get much kick taking pot shots at a squirrel. He packed, again, and headed for Chicago.

For a few years he floated. Then one night in a bad section of St. Louis a man started a fight and pulled a knife on Garrison. Ray took it away from him and broke the blade on the bar top. Then, with his hands, he beat the other man to death.

The police didn't get there in time. They'd been nowhere near the place and by the time they got there Ray was in a fat man's apartment. The man told Garrison he was okay, there was work for someone like him. He asked Garrison was he good with a gun and Garrison just smiled.

That's ancient history, he thought now, the car hugging the road and heading south from Tampa. Ancient history. All those years with the mob, all those syndicate jobs for fast, clean cash, they were done with. The syndicate wanted too much. They wanted to own you, and Garrison didn't want to be owned. So he worked freelance now. He worked for whoever hired him, did an average of four jobs a year, at an average of five grand a job. When not on an assignment, which was ninety percent of the time, he loafed. He floated around the country, stayed in good hotels, read Rimbaud. He liked Rimbaud.

He was in Key West in the morning. The little island was quiet, warm. He parked the car in a field, unlocked the trunk, broke down the high-powered rifle and packed it in his suitcase with his clothes. He went through his wallet, destroyed the few pieces of identification made out to David Palmer. He didn't need the car now, didn't need Palmer. He picked up the suitcase and lugged it down the main street of the town. He stopped at a restaurant for breakfast, ate a double order of ham and eggs and drank a quart of cold milk.

The counterman was short and bald. "I want to charter a boat," Garrison told him.

"Fishing?"

Garrison shrugged. "A speedy little launch. Something quick and easy. Who do I see?"

The counterman thought about it. "Try Phil Di Angelo," he suggested. "You can most times find him down at the fourth pier, or at the Blue Moon, it's a bar down there."

Garrison thanked him and left. He tried the docks and didn't find Di Angelo. In the Blue Moon the bartender pointed to a dark, unshaven man sitting alone with a bottle of beer at a table in the back. Garrison carried his suitcase across the dirty floor and sat down near Di Angelo. The man looked up. He had been drinking, Garrison saw, but he was not drunk.

"You've got a boat for hire," Garrison said.

Di Angelo looked at him. "You wanta hire her?"

"I might. Is she fast?"

"Fast and trim. The fishing's so-so now, not too good and not too bad. You won't get a sail, if that's what you're looking for. No sail and no tarpon. We might have some fun."

"I don't fish."

"No?" Di Angelo's eyes were shrewd, appraising. "Go on, man."

Garrison said "I want to go to Cuba. Havana."

"You crazy?"

"No."

"You must be crazy."

Garrison didn't say anything. He waited for Di Angelo to make up his mind.

"I could do it, man. It'll cost you."

"How much?"

"A grand."

Garrison sighed. He stood up and started to leave.

"Hey—"

"It's too much," he said.

"How much, then?"

"Half," Garrison said. "Five hundred, no more."

Di Angelo tried to haggle but it didn't work. "All right," he said finally. "When do we leave?"

"Tomorrow."

"Jesus, it takes time. It takes a hell of a time. You can't just—"

"It's a ninety-mile trip and it takes a couple of hours. Cut the crap."

"There's boats," Di Angelo said desperately. "Patrol boats, ours and theirs. You can't just dodge them."

"You're going to fly over their heads?"

For a few more minutes they sat and stared at each other. Then Di Angelo said: "All right, you're paying for it. But not tomorrow. Tonight, at midnight. I don't want to go in daylight. Tonight at midnight or it's no deal."

"It's a deal," Garrison said.

The house in Ybor City was comfortable. Matt Garth sat in front of the television set for two days. He drank beer from cans and smoked Cuban cigars. He also kept an eye on Fenton, who was some kind of a nut. Here they were, living it up big, eating good food and doing nothing much, and Fenton kept hopping around like a dog with fleas. He had a good thing going and he was too dumb to know it.

"Look," Garth would tell him, "cool off, have a beer, calm down. This is fine, right? We wait until they take us to that plane. Then we do what we do. You scared or something?"

"I'm not scared."

"Then cool it. Relax. We don't go up against this Castro guy for a while yet. The longer we sit here, the better. There's time."

"No," Fenton would say. "There's no time at all. There's very little time, Mr. Garth."

"You could call me Matt."

"Matt, then."

"What do I call you? Earl?"

"Whatever you like," Fenton said.

So Garth didn't bother after that. He went on drinking cans of beer and smoking good Cuban cigars and thinking about Castro, the guy they were supposed to hit. It didn't make sense to him but he wasn't going to waste his time worrying about what made sense and what didn't. That wasn't the sort of thing he busted his mind over. He was an easygoing type, a guy who had more muscles than brains and knew it. He valued his brawn because plenty of guys with brains had paid him when they needed muscle to get a job done for them.

He worked for anyone who had the money to hire him, spent his earnings as soon as they came in, and drifted from one job to another without a worry. He had done a short bit for aggravated assault once in Dannemora, a few light stretches for drunk-and-disorderly and things like that, and since then he had learned to cool it when it came to the law. Outside of that, he had a simple and lazy moral and ethical code. He looked out for Number One, played it straight as a die with whoever was picking up the tab, and generally managed to come out of things right side up.

He had been a strike breaker, an enforcer, a bouncer, had done almost anything requiring the talents of somebody who could hit hard and swing freely. He was tougher than hell—two teeth were gone in front from a cop's nightstick, and he had taken that same cop and put him in the hospital for a few months. That was the bit that sent him to Dannemora. But before they tried him the police worked him over, slammed him around some to avenge the cop in the hospital. He took everything they handed him. He never yelled and he never put in a gripe. He took it and they couldn't break him.

Now, because some Cuban nut was on speaking terms with one of the heavies who had hired him before, he was going to Cuba to get this Castro. He didn't know who Castro was, except that he was running Cuba and somebody didn't want him to keep on with it. He didn't care about this. He cared about twenty grand, which meant soft living for a long time. Twenty grand could get you into a lot of big-breasted girls. You could drink a lot of premium beer, sleep in a lot of silk-sheeted beds.

So what the hell.

On the third day, a car came for them. The driver was a light-skinned Negro with cold eyes. He drove them out of Tampa, down the Tamiami Trail, to the airstrip. Garth noticed that Fenton seemed excited. Scared, he decided. Maybe scared the plane'll crash. And Garth laughed.

The plane was a twin-engine Cessna, a little puddle-jumper. The Negro told Garth and Fenton that there were supplies for them on the plane, that the pilot could tell them what they wanted to know. The Negro drove away. They got into the plane and the pilot warmed up the engines, taxied down a very small runway and took off.

"You like flying?" he asked Fenton.

"I don't mind it."

"I can take it or not," Garth said. "He said something about supplies. Let's have a look, huh?"

The supplies were guns, ammunition, some minor explosives. Garth looked them over and whistled. "We better not hit anything coming down," he said. "Gunpowder and dynamite. We'd go up like a bomb."

"I wouldn't worry," Fenton told him. "The pilot seems to know what he's doing."

"Yeah?"

"Yes."

The pilot knew what he was doing. He flew north of Cuba, skirting the big island and coming in over the Bahamas, then cutting south to fly over Acklins Island and move in on Oriente Province, the easternmost section of Cuba. It was hill country there, rough jungle land with dense vegetation and jagged terrain. Guerrilla fighters could disappear in that sort of country. Castro, with a force of only twelve men, had started in the Oriente hills. His twelve men had lasted, had been reinforced, until they had pushed Batista off the island and had sent him running for his life.

But now time had played tricks. Now Castro was in Havana, growing sleek with power, and other rebel bands roamed the hills of Oriente. Small bands, hiding, fighting in desperate skirmishes.

The plane flew over Cuba. Garth didn't even see the landing strip until they were almost on the ground. He couldn't understand how the pilot had managed to find it. They landed in a cleared portion of a farmer's tiny field. The pilot had killed the engine long ago. The air was still, warm.

Three men and a woman rushed to meet the plane as Garth and Fenton climbed down from it. The men carried drawn revolvers; the woman had a rifle across one shoulder. Two of the men went to unload the Cessna. The other, with the woman, came to Fenton and Garth.

"You are the Americans from Señor Hiraldo?" the man asked.

"That is correct," Fenton said. Garth remained silent, his eyes looking at the woman. She was maybe twenty-five, maybe younger. Her hair was long and uncombed, her eyes dark brown. She wore a pair of khaki pants and a torn army field jacket. The clothing couldn't hide the shape of her body. Her breasts were large and firm, her hips ideal for bearing children or making love. Garth stared at her and wanted her.

"I am called Manuel," the man said. "The others, my comrades, have no English. I have some English. I speak not well, I fear."

"You speak very well," Fenton said.

"You have much kindness. But we must hurry. There is little time for pleasantness in the hills. Soldiers are everywhere."

The other two men ran off, their arms filled with guns, ammunition and explosives. Manuel and the woman were behind them, Garth and Fenton close on their heels. Already the pilot was warming up the plane, anxious to get out of Cuba in a hurry.

Garth watched the girl. He lumbered through the brush with thorns snatching at his clothing but all he could think of was the girl, the way she walked. He saw her buttocks moving within the khaki pants. He wondered if she wore underwear.

He was going to have her.

He knew this, knew it for a fact. The broad was hotter than hell, he thought, and he was going to get her on her back if it was the last thing he did. If she was sold on the idea, fine and dandy. If she wanted to put out, swell. That made it easier, and why take the tough way?

But it was all up to her. Because one way or the other he was going to get in her pants, whether she liked it or not, whether she was somebody's wife or somebody's sister or somebody's mother, it didn't make a damned bit of difference. If it had to be rape that's what it was going to be. It was up to her.

The underbrush got progressively thicker and Garth waded through it like a rhinoceros charging through savannah grasses. The guy called Manuel was keeping up a running stream of chatter but Garth wasn't listening. He was busy watching the broad.

Some party, he thought. And for this they were paying him twenty grand!

The boat took Turner and Hines to a coral reef hedging a broad bay. There a man met their ship in a rowboat. Turner and Hines joined the man and he put them ashore just outside Matanzas.

Matanzas is a commercial port on the north coast of Cuba, some thirty-six miles due east of Havana. The city's name means *slaughter* in Spanish. Turner knew enough Spanish to get along. Slaughter, he thought. Not murder, not assassination. Slaughter. He wondered who was going to get slaughtered.

He found out in a hurry. The man beached the rowboat and joined them on shore. He was leading them to the Bellamar Caves, a group of limestone caverns three miles outside of Matanzas. There they would spend the night.

"Manos arriba!" The voice was loud, sharp. Turner whirled around, flung his hands up in response to the command. There were two tall men across the road,

both bearded, both uniformed. One held a pistol.

They dogtrotted across the road, eyes bright. This was it, then, Turner thought. They had entered illegally, and Castro's men had them already.

The man with the gun was talking now, gesticulating wildly, demanding in rapid Spanish who they were and what they were doing. The Cuban who had rowed them in looked frightened. Hines was standing numb, his hands high in the air.

Turner waited. His muscles tensed. He looked at the gun. It was pointed between him and Hines now. The soldier was getting careless.

Turner sprang.

One hand closed on the soldier's wrist, driving the gun down. His other hand clenched into a fist that connected solidly with the side of the soldier's head. The man reeled backward, and now everybody was getting into the act. Hines and the Cuban were on the other soldier—they had him before he had a chance to get his gun from its holster. Turner was on his man, pounding his head down against the road, beating the man to death.

It was short, and very bloody. It was a fight conducted in silence, a battle from a silent movie. It ended with two bearded soldiers lying dead in the road. Turner stood up, drained, every muscle aching. He saw Hines with his nose bleeding. The Cuban had a huge welt on his forehead, another welt on one cheek.

"This is bad," the man said in Spanish.

Turner nodded.

"They will know we have been here. They will find these men dead and they will wonder what has happened."

"Can we get rid of the bodies?"

The Cuban thought for a moment. Suddenly he smiled. "Help me with them," he said. "I shall take them in the rowboat. I shall take them far out, and they will be buried at sea with full naval honors."

"Won't they be missed?"

The Cuban shrugged. "Many soldiers desert," he said. "Many leave the country. These will be deserters."

Turner and Hines helped the Cuban with the bodies. They waited in the darkness while the man rowed out to sea in the small boat. It seemed to take forever before he returned, the boat empty of human cargo now.

"It is done," he said. "Let us go. Quickly."

He led them now to Bellamar. Guides led visitors through the limestone grottoes, but these guides went off duty at eight in the evening and did not return until seven in the morning. Hines and Turner were led through a cavern, along an underground trail. There were no lights. After a long stretch of darkness the Cuban flicked on a pocket flash and they could see where they were going.

They spent the night deep in the heart of Bellamar, far past the point where guides led *turistas*. There, four other men sat around a fire on which a pot of chili beans and rice was cooking slowly. Turner and Hines ate the beans and rice and drank wine from a jug. A sad-eyed Cuban strummed an out-of-tune guitar and sang songs.

The catacombs, Turner thought. A batch of crazy Christians hiding from the Romans. He took a long drink of wine and remembered the night before they had boarded the boat, the night in Miami, the rare steaks and the Canadian Club and the two hustlers. It had been good for the kid, for Hines. It had taken some of the tension out of his eyes. That was good.

And it had been good for Turner. First the steaks, prime strip sirloins fresh from the broiler. They had been burned on the outside and raw in the middle, the way steak should always be. The Canadian Club was good to wash the food down with, and the girls were there by the time the meal was done.

Two girls. One was a redhead and the other a blonde, and what the hell difference did it make if they had started life with the same shade of mouse-brown hair? They were a redhead and a blonde now. The redhead was a little taller, and the blonde's breasts were a little larger, and they both knew as much about love-making as anyone else in the world. Maybe more.

It started out as a party, with the bottle passing from mouth to mouth, with the four of them sitting on the long couch and getting happily gassed. It finished up as an orgy, a full-blown orgy, a pretty fine way for Hines to lose his virginity. He lost it on the floor with the blonde at about the same time that Turner was enjoying the redhead on the couch.

Then they had traded off. And then they traded back, and at one point Turner watched with clinical detachment while the blonde and the redhead made love to Hines at the same time, the young novice jumping from one to the other with great agility, keeping both girls whimpering and thrashing. And, since turnabout was only fair play, then it had been his turn with both girls.

A good evening. A valuable evening, because all the liquor and all the lust made time run away, made death and murder and pursuit take a back seat to more immediate sensual excesses. And that was vital; you had to forget murder now and then or you went out of your mind.

Murder. Assassination. Killing. Slaughter. Matanzas.

The wine made sleep come in a hurry. Turner woke up around six. Hines was shaking him awake.

"We're supposed to get out of here," the kid was saying. "The guides come on in an hour. We have to leave before they start or we're stuck here until to-night."

Turner shook himself awake. He had slept in his clothes and he felt grimy. He sucked on his teeth, coughed, spat out phlegm. He found a crumpled cigarette in a shirt pocket and lit it. The smoke helped him wake up.

He yawned and stretched. Moreno, the sad-eyed guitar player of the night before, was the only Cuban who was awake. The others lay sleeping around the ashes of the campfire. They were all hunted men, Turner knew. They stayed in the caves all of the time. Moreno grinned quickly and passed the wine jug to Turner. Turner took a long swallow, offered the jug to Hines. The kid shook his head and Turner had another drink. He was awake now. It was time to get going.

"*A donde vamos?*" he asked Moreno. "Where are we going?"

"Habana."

"*Como?*" he asked. "How? On foot?"

Moreno told them in Spanish simply to come, to follow. He led them out of the caves again. Turner decided that he could not possibly have found his way alone. He wondered how Moreno managed it. One cave looked pretty much like the next.

"The underground," he told Hines. "They don't kid around here. The underground lives under the ground."

They were out of the caves finally and Turner took his first look at Cuba by daylight. The sun was bright, the sky empty of clouds. The air, while warmish, was clear and fresh, especially after the stale air of the caverns. He filled his lungs with it, killed his cigarette. Moreno had a car parked nearby and Turner and Hines got into the back seat. In Spanish Moreno said that he was going to drive them into Havana.

"Just like that?"

Moreno said it was simple, that no one would stop the car. He was taking them to the home of some members of the underground, he explained. These members were not known to the police. There was a room in the basement, a safe room, and Turner and Hines would live there. They would be fed, they would have beds to sleep in. And from there they could murder the Communist bastard Castro, the betrayer of revolutions, the murderer of women and children, the pig, the *ladron*, the *hijo de la gran puta*, the *maricon*, the *hombre sin cojones*—

All of this came in a steady stream that sounded as though it had been memorized from a prepared speech. Turner didn't bother listening to the end of it. It was more fun looking out the window.

The highway between Matanzas and Havana had been built within the past several years and looked it. It was wide and traffic moved at a steady pace. The cars, Turner noticed, were mostly old ones. Almost all were American models, with an occasional Volkswagen and Renault tossed in. The newest one Turner spotted was a Fifty-eight Buick. The road ran parallel to the shore but a good distance away from it. There were cane fields on both sides, fields broken by an occasional gas station or roadside restaurant.

Turner glanced at Hines. The kid was looking out the window, too. "It's pretty," he said.

"You sound surprised."

"It's not what I expected."

"What did you have in mind? Guns and barbed wire?"

"Something like that."

Turner shrugged. "I don't know politics," he said. "They don't interest me. But I've been a few places, done a few things. I used to ship out, short term cargo stuff, up and down the coast and around the gulf."

"I know."

"You meet people, sailors. That's where I picked up Spanish. I've shipped with Cubans. It's not that bad down here, Jim."

"You think Castro's a bargain?"

"I think he's a bastard and a son-of-a-bitch. He found a little power and it went to his head. This happens. But Batista was just as big a bastard. The average Joe didn't eat steak and still doesn't. A few years ago he had to be satisfied with beans and rice and was happy to get that. One revolution later and he's still eating the same crap. They've got wholesale executions and no democracy and it's easy to find a lot of reasons to put Castro down. But you get back to the average Joe and he doesn't care about these reasons. He's more interested in eating better and being pushed around less. And all the things he finds wrong he can sit back and blame the Yankees for them, because that's what Loudmouth Castro tells him, over and over again, *ad nauseam*. He figures Castro and the people around him are Communists but he also figures he's got nothing to lose. So don't look around for barbed wire. They don't need it yet. The average Joe is still on Castro's side or, at least, not definitely against him."

"How about the underground? Aren't they average Joes, Turner?"

"No. Maybe they're rebels, sharp guys with a yen for more and better. Maybe they want power on their own. Hell, maybe they're crooks or nuts or cranks or rapists or—"

Hines pointed to the driver.

"Forget him. He doesn't understand English. None of the gang at the cave understood English."

"How do you know?"

"I tested them last night. I told them all to go home and drop dead. They didn't even frown. We'll be getting into Havana pretty soon. What do you think of the setup?"

"It sounds okay."

"Yeah? Maybe it does, I don't know. The way it looks from here, we got quite a little game to play. Our boy'll be guarded six ways and backwards. I don't know about you, but I want to get out of this alive. I'm in it for the dough."

"I'm in it for revenge." said Hines. "But it's not revenge if you get yourself killed in the bargain. Ever read *The Cask of Amontillado* by Poe?"

"No."

"Oh," Hines said. "It's a short story. About revenge. One guy seals another guy in a wall in a wine cellar, just seals him in alive and leaves him there. Anyway, one of the lines says that in order to make revenge come off you have to get away with it."

"I'll go along with that," Turner said. "But I don't think we can seal our boy in a wine cellar. How are you with a gun?"

"I don't know. I never used one."

"Not even in ROTC?"

Hines colored. "I managed to cop out of that. I brought a note from my doctor telling them I was a bed-wetter. I'm not, really, I just—"

Turner laughed out loud. "Oh, to hell with it," he said. "I used to be fair with a rifle but it's been a long time. And you have to be lucky. There'll be a crowd around and taking a pot shot at Castro would be like buying a lottery ticket. That much chance of it working. I was thinking about a bomb."

"A bomb?"

"The homemade kind, the kind you throw. We'll blow him to hell and then figure out a way to get home. How does it sound?"

"It sounds fine," Hines said. "I guess."

Turner rolled down the window next to him and flipped out his cigarette. Hines said something, some conversational feeler, but he didn't bother listening or answering. He didn't feel like talking any more.

They were hitting the outskirts of Havana now, passing through middle-class suburbs. Turner saw Morro Castle on the right, La Cubana fortress on the left. Then there was the bridge, a wide modern span across the strait separating Havana Bay from the ocean. And they were in the city.

It was a city, he thought. It could have been part of New York or Philly or Charleston or San Diego. It didn't feel foreign. The people in the streets were Cuban and the signs were in Spanish, but there were neighborhoods like that all over the States—Spic Harlem in New York, Ybor City in Tampa, Mex Town in San Diego. Hell, the neighborhood here was a little poorer, the people were more down at the heels. But Spanish Harlem and Ybor City weren't exactly the Ritz.

He noticed a prostitute soliciting, a cop ignoring her. "I heard Castro closed the whorehouses," he said to Moreno in Spanish. "Made hustling against the law."

"There are still prostitutes," Moreno said.

"I figured there were. She didn't look like a nun."

Moreno managed a shrug, an expressive one. "There will always be *putas*," he said.

"Yeah. Well, thank God for that."

"You wish to meet a girl?"

He laughed. "No," he said. "I'm just a sightseer. This place of yours much farther?"

It wasn't. Moreno turned a corner into La Avenida de Sangre and pulled up at the curb. *The Avenue of Blood,* Turner thought. *And Matanzas meant slaughter. Christ on wheels.*

The house Moreno led them to was a two-story frame dwelling. It needed paint. There was a front porch, and an old man rocked on it in silence, a thin black cigar in his mouth. His eyes looked up sleepily, then looked away.

"He is old and quiet," Moreno said. "*El Viejo*, the old one. Toothless and harmless, no? You may see that his hand is inside the jacket of his suit. There is a gun in his hand. He knows me. Otherwise you would have been shot before you entered this house."

"I'm impressed," Turner said.

The door opened. A woman, stout and matronly, smiled benignly at them. She stepped inside, murmured something polite and let them pass. She had hair the color of a gray flannel suit. A thin scar ran from the corner of her mouth halfway to her eye. It looked to Turner as though it had been made by a knife. Moreno introduced her as Señora Luchar. She mumbled something pleasant again and went off to find coffee. She brought a tray of demitasse cups that were small without being dainty. The coffee was very thick, very hot, very black. Turner liked it.

Moreno finished his coffee and left. He took a long time to finish the coffee and a longer time to leave. He kept speaking in Spanish to the woman, telling her how important the task of the two Americans was, telling her to render them all possible assistance. The woman—Señora Luchar—listened to all of this with no expression. Finally Moreno was gone. Señora Luchar followed him to the door, bolted it, watched the man drive away.

"Un momento, Señora—"

She turned to Turner. "Let's speak English," she said briskly. "Your accent is impossible. What's on your mind?"

"Uh—"

"Moreno's a fool," she said. "A useful fool, but still a fool. You didn't know I spoke English? I lived in Miami, for five years. Political exile. My family didn't get along with Batista. His men pulled out my old man's finger-nails. They cut off his testicles, gouged out his eyes, raped my mother and slit her throat. They raped me, too, but they let me go."

"And now you want to kill Castro?"

"I don't like dictators. Fascist or Marxist, I don't like dictators. You two sleep in the cellar. Want to see your room? Follow me."

They followed her.

four

July 26, 1953.

With his briefs ignored by Batista's courts, with freedom of speech and freedom of the press forcibly suppressed throughout Cuba, Fidel Castro decided that only revolution would settle the issues at stake— the issues of freedom and liberty. He began meeting with friends in an apartment house in the Vedado district of Havana, planning a military operation which would excite the common people of Cuba and spark a revolt to send Fulgencio Batista running from the island.

The revolutionaries were a small group, a tiny band of idealists and heroes, and, some say, Communists. Ambassador William Pauley has stated on the Jack Paar Show that he heard Castro, very early in his career, proclaim that when it came it would be a Communist revolution. The capital at their disposal was minimal. The men themselves mortgaged their homes, sold their furniture, pawned their watches and their wives' jewelry, gave up whatever they had in order to place as much money as possible at Castro's disposal. They armed themselves with pistols and knives; some carried rifles and shotguns. They had no grenades, no explosives. They were, in all, a total force of one hundred seventy men. Their objective, initially, was the fortress at Moncada at Santiago, a fortress quartering somewhere in the neighborhood of fifteen hundred armed troops.

Castro set out for Santiago by automobile and stayed at a friend's house in the center of the city. On July 25th, more of the revolutionaries began drifting east, converging on the city. Fidel met with them at ten that night, coordinating the attack, synchronizing plans.

The attack commenced the next morning. The revolutionaries moved through Santiago in groups. One task force was dispatched to capture the radio station, preparing to call upon the people of Santiago to join in the revolt and take arms against the government. Another group moved to occupy the Santiago hospital, to hold it in preparation for the care of wounded on both sides. The major group launched an onslaught against the Moncada Fortress.

But the uprising, nobly conceived and fearlessly put into execution, was smashed almost at once. Castro's little band was undermanned and under-equipped. The radio station was not taken, and the bulk of the citizens of the town were not aware that a rebellion was in progress until it had already been put down.

At Moncada, Castro's followers fought staunchly in the face of impossible odds, but they were too thoroughly outnumbered to have much effect. Batista's army retained control, and the rebels scattered for their lives.

Many were killed in the fighting. Others, captured, never reached prison; they were killed on the spot by Batista's troops. Fidel himself, and his younger brother Raul as well, narrowly missed execution in this manner. Only because the army officer who captured him had been a classmate of his at Havana was he delivered to the civilian authorities instead of being put to death at once.

Castro acted as his own attorney in the trial held that September. He told the court that an attorney appointed by the Havana Bar Association had not been permitted to see him while he was in jail, that he himself had been denied access to documents important to his defense. Nevertheless he made an impassioned and eloquent plea to the court, lashing out against the excesses of the Batista regime, presenting his projected reforms, criticizing the inequality and oppression which he saw around him throughout Cuba. His defense, doomed from the start, since the courts were in Batista's hands, was not successful. It had no chance.

But his speech was successful. People listened to the tall young man with the firm voice. People who had never known Castro existed began to take him into their hearts as a leader. The trial, designed by Batista to squelch the resistance forever, had an opposite effect. It increased Castro's following. And Fidel himself saw with greater confidence something he had already learned at the University of Havana: when he spoke, Cubans listened.

"I end my defense," he told the court, "but I shall not do it as lawyers always do, asking for the defendant's liberty. I cannot ask for this when my companions are already suffering imprisonment on the Isle of Pines. Send me to join them and to share their fate. It is inconceivable that honest men are dead or jailed in a republic unless the President is a criminal or thief.

"As for me, I know that jail will be hard as it has never been for anyone else, pregnant with threats and with cowardly ferociousness. But I do not fear it as I do not fear the fury of the wretched tyrant who has already torn away the life of seventy brothers.

"Condemn me! It does not matter! History will absolve me!"

The judges may or may not have been impressed; there is no way to tell. But, whether or not history would absolve Fidel Castro, they had no intention of so doing. He was sentenced to fifteen years in prison on the Isle of Pines.

Prison can be an end or a beginning. For Fidel, the time spent on the Isle of Pines was not time to be wasted. With Raul and his other comrades in arms, he maintained strict revolutionary discipline, sang songs of rebellion and planned for the future. Castro organized a school in prison, teaching his fellow prisoners history and philosophy. The cheers and loyalty of followers was something he was accustomed to now, something he needed. He would drive himself to im-

possible extremes to serve those persons who, he felt, were counting on him.

But his activities with his fellow prisoners only aggravated the government. He was isolated, made to serve what amounted to solitary confinement. Still the young man from Oriente refused to waste his time. He read constantly, poring over every book he could get on Cuban history and the age-old fight for Cuban independence. He waited for his release from prison and planned a rise to power.

It was May of 1955 before Batista ultimately gave in to outside pressure and granted amnesty to the political prisoners on the Isle of Pines. At last Castro was released, returned with Raul by boat to Havana. He prepared to enter politics once more. Batista was attempting to preserve a front of honest elections while holding the reins of power as tightly as ever, and friends presumed that Fidel could now climb to power by legal means. But Castro knew better.

He tried to make speeches, and found that radio time was closed to him. He sent letters to the newspapers and they were never printed. Throughout Cuba he saw nothing but oppression, nothing but the hand of a dictator. And he decided once more that he had been right the first time, that revolution was the only method of ridding Cuba of a dictator.

He went to Mexico. His wife, the sister of an ardent Batistiano, had already deserted him; now she divorced him. He had no money and little support, only his image burning in the hearts of silent Cubans. He found a man named Bayo who had led guerrilla forces in the Spanish Civil War and persuaded Bayo to help him train an army of rebels. He went through Spanish America, through the United States, struggling to raise money and forces.

He had failed once, attacking Moncada. He did not intend to fail again.

five

Earl Fenton sat with his back against a scrub pine and his Sten gun across his knees. He sat still, very still, and he wished for a cigarette. A little tube of paper filled with rolled tobacco, a little paper-and-tobacco affair that you could light with a match and smoke quickly. In his mind he could taste the brisk jolt of strong smoke taken deep into his sick lungs. He could taste it and feel it.

There was a pack of cigarettes in the pocket of his field jacket. There were matches, too. All he had to do was take a cigarette, scratch a match, put the two together and smoke. But you didn't smoke when the Castristas were less than fifty yards away. You didn't send up gray clouds to tip your hand. Instead you put your back against the trunk of a tree, set your gun across your knees. And you waited.

The soldiers—five of them, maybe six—were at the shoulder of the road on the other side of a dense growth of shrubbery. They had come in a noisy, gear-grinding Jeep and they were looking for rebels. Fenton could not see them from where he sat, but he had caught glimpses of them before, one with a full Fidel-style beard, one young and crisply smooth-shaven, a driver wearing opaque sunglasses, two or three others. And now it would be very easy to take a step or two and put the Sten gun to use. He could get one, two, maybe three of them before he was shot.

But that wasn't good enough. Manuel, leader of the group, had explained all that. If you killed three men and then were killed yourself, you had the worst of the bargain. And they didn't know for sure that the soldiers were looking for these particular rebels. Maybe somebody had tipped them off, maybe not.

"We must first survive," Manuel had said. "They are many, we are few. To risk a life is not to be a hero. It is enough to be here, to be a hero. They can afford to have fifty, a hundred, five hundred men killed. When they kill a single one of us, it is a big loss."

So self-protection came first. They would make no move until the soldiers made it necessary. They would sit quietly by and if the Castristas drove away, so much the better. Their job was to kill Castro, not his followers. That's what they were being paid for. Even the Cubans with them realized this made good sense.

Fenton breathed shallowly and thought about cigarettes. How long had it been? Two days, five days? Somewhere in the middle, and he could not be sure of the time, could not tell because time moved differently here. It was not measured in eight-hour shifts as it had been at the Metropolitan Bank of Lynbrook. It was tricky.

Time. Fenton looked over at Garth, his great bulk

crouched in the shadows of twisted, bright-leaved trees. Garth, too, held a Sten gun. Garth had killed before, he knew. And now he, Fenton, was a killer also. They had stumbled into Castristas before and Fenton had killed, had sent bullets screaming into bodies. He still remembered vividly the Sten gun bucking like an unbroken horse in his hands, but in the end the men had gone down with bullets in their flesh. And, by God, Fenton had outlived them. Fenton, Earl Fenton, a dying man—

Footsteps. He heard movement, the soldiers poking at the roadside brush with their rifles, getting ready to move around. Any moment now. He looked from Garth to Manuel, cool and sharp and aware. Then to Taco Sardo, the sixteen-year-old who spoke only Spanish and rarely spoke that. And then the girl, Maria, the one Garth was constantly bothering, the silent broody-eyed girl who accused the world with her voiceless stare. Strange that her name was Maria. Like the girl in the Hemingway novel, the novel about the bridge. She was not at all like that fictional Maria. And yet the exterior trappings were similar.

More footsteps. He saw Garth straighten up, saw Maria raise her gun and brace herself. Manuel was moving to a vantage point and Taco was following his lead. Fenton knew the procedure. Manuel would fire the first shot if the searcher got too close, and then the rest of them would begin. Manuel would wait for the right moment.

The tension was flooding his limbs now, tension and excitement that spread through his cells as cancer had spread through his lungs. Fenton got to his feet silently, crept forward, propped himself up on a boulder and sighted over the top. He could see them now. There were six. Three of them poked at the brush like idiots. The bearded one was looking in another direction through a pair of binoculars. The driver with the dark glasses was behind the wheel of the Jeep. A sixth crouched in the road. He was tying his shoelaces.

Slowly, silently, the rebels moved in. The gap was closed by ten yards, fifteen yards. The Sten gun, handy as it was, worked poorly at long range. You did better in close.

Fenton stopped, dropped to one knee. He sighted in on the driver, the one with the sunglasses. He had to be hit right away, Fenton decided. Or he would simply hit the gas pedal and get away. Why let him get away?

The man in the road finished tying his shoelaces. He straightened up, turned toward the Jeep. Then something stopped him and he turned, his eyes darting like a sparrow. He had spotted movement in the bushes and he rushed forward, his gun at the ready.

Manuel shot him through the chest.

Then all hell broke loose. Fenton squeezed the trigger and let the Sten gun leap and chatter in his hands. His first burst was wide, smashing the Jeep's windshield, but his second burst took half the driver's head away. The man slumped over the wheel and died.

Garth and Maria had drilled two of the soldiers in their tracks. The bearded one and another were behind the Jeep, returning fire.

Fenton sent a burst at the Jeep, hoping for the gas tank. He missed. A bullet whined over his head and he flattened out, staying close to the ground, holding tight to his gun. Taco Sardo was a short distance to the left. He was trying to circle around, to move in on the two Castristas from the side. Maria was creeping off in the opposite direction. It was a pincer movement, Fenton realized. A spontaneous, intuitive pincer movement, carried out on an individual basis rather than by regiments or battalions.

He heard heavy breathing to one side. It was Garth, moving closer, face flushed with combat fever, eyes stupid but determined. Fenton jammed a fresh clip into the breech of his gun and tried several more rounds on the gas tank of the Jeep. He saw Taco on the left, then heard a quick, sharp rifle shot from the rear of the Jeep. Taco went down, moaning, clutching at his leg.

Then a Sten gun, an answering Sten gun. Maria, far on the right, surprising the two soldiers with hot lead. One died with a bullet in his throat. The other, the one with the beard, threw down his rifle and stretched his hands toward the sky.

Now they moved in, all of them. This also called for speed, for guerrilla tactics, for expediency. Manuel and Fenton checked each soldier in turn, made sure the five bodies on the ground were corpses. Maria held her gun on the bearded one. Garth went to check on Taco, then came back.

"The kid's all right," he told Manuel. "He got it in the leg. The bleeding ain't bad and the bone's okay. I can lug him back and he'll be walking tomorrow."

Manuel nodded shortly. Now the bearded soldier was talking, pleading for his life. He did not sound frightened at all. His voice was calm, rational. There were beads of perspiration dotting his forehead but those were the only signs of worry.

"He wishes us to let him to live," Manuel said in English. "He says he will make no trouble for us. He says not to kill him."

The bearded man spoke again.

"He says one more death will accomplish nothing," Manuel translated. "And so we should let him live. So he may return and kill us all."

The bearded soldier started to protest; evidently he understood English. Manuel's eyes hardened. He lowered his Sten gun, took a pistol from his cartridge belt. The soldier's eyes widened and his mouth opened. Manuel very deliberately placed the mouth of the pistol against the soldier's forehead and spattered his brains over the trunk of the car.

They piled the six bodies into the Jeep. There was a container of spare gasoline in the trunk. Fenton unscrewed the cap, poured the gasoline over the bodies and over the Jeep. He stepped back, took out a cigarette, scratched a match. He took two long drags on

the cigarette and pitched the butt underhand into the
Jeep. It was safer that way, easier than tossing a match.
The gasoline went up with a roar and the Jeep was
transformed into a sheet of flame.

They left in a hurry. They collected weapons, ammunition. Garth shouldered Taco like a sack of dirty
laundry and the rest of them followed him into the
woods. Fenton brought up the rear, his heart still
pounding, the excitement still a living force.

Another victory. Six men dead this time, six corpses
baking in a burning Jeep. It was bloody, it was the
supreme insult to a corpse, but he knew that it had
been necessary.

Fenton walked and death walked with him. Death
always walked with him now, a thin pain in the chest
that was always close at hand. And it was strange to
have death as a companion. Before, when he lived with
no fear of death, no sure foreknowledge of doom, it had
been enough simply to live, to exist, to go on.

Now it was different. Now he enjoyed killing, killing,
killing. It was the only way to prove that he was still
alive.

It was a Thursday night and Garrison was eating in the
best restaurant in Havana. The restaurant was Le Ven-
dome, on Calle Calzado, and the food was French.
Garrison had baked clams, chateaubriand, and a small
bottle of Bordeaux Rouge. He passed up dessert and
had cognac with his coffee.

When he had finished he paid his check, left a tip, and walked out of the restaurant. He looked neat and summery in his cord suit. His tie was neatly knotted, his shoes polished. He walked with a sure, easy stride. Outside, he let the doorman summon a cab for him, pressed a coin into the man's palm, settled into his seat and told the driver to drop him at the Nacional. That was his hotel, the city's oldest and one of its best, completely air-conditioned, well serviced, with bars and a pool and a night club and a gambling casino. Tourists were still allowed to gamble in Castro's Cuba, but Cuban nationals were prohibited from doing so. This amused Garrison.

He got out at the Nacional, tipped the driver, strode into the lobby and took an elevator to his room. Inside it, with the door locked and bolted, he made a quick check of the room. It had been searched again, he noted, amused. And once again they had failed to find either gun. The rifle was still in his mattress—he had slashed the mattress cover, wedged the gun into the ticking and sewed the mattress up again. The Beretta was still inside the television set where he had placed it. It didn't even interfere with the operation of the TV. Not that he cared, he never bothered turning it on. All you ever got were Fidel's speeches, and it wasn't hard to get tired of them. He said the same thing all the time and took six hours each time to say it.

Garrison undressed, went into the bathroom and adjusted the shower spray. He showered quickly, shaved, trimmed his mustache. Then he stretched out on his bed and closed his eyes.

This was the easy way. He wondered where the others were, Fenton and Turner and Garth and Hines. Probably crouching in a dirty little room somewhere with a batch of grubby Cubans mumbling at them. And this was so much simpler. Just the direct method, quick and easy.

He'd had to get to Cuba illegally, in Di Angelo's boat. That much was easy enough. And then there was that shrewd old Cuban on La Avenida Blanca, the one a New Orleans contact had put him wise to. You didn't need a passport or a visa to stay in Cuba. All you needed was an identification paper and they gave you that as you got off the boat. And that little old man had given him one that couldn't look more like the real thing. You didn't even need the damned thing while you were *in* Cuba—nobody ever asked for it—but you had to have it to leave the country. And Garrison planned to leave the country the day Castro died.

His eyes opened. He grinned, looked at the ceiling, closed his eyes again. The simple way. He was an American businessman on vacation, a real estate speculator who occasionally took a taxi to look at a piece of property. He stayed in a top hotel, ate at good restaurants, tipped a shade too heavily, drank a little too much, and didn't speak a damned word of Spanish. Hardly an assassin, or a secret agent, or anything of the sort. They searched his room, of course, but this happened

regularly in every Latin American country. It was a
matter of form. Actually, it tended to reassure him,
since they searched so clumsily that he knew they were
not afraid of him. Otherwise they would take pains to
be more subtle.

The simple way. He stood up, naked and hard-
muscled, and walked to his window. He'd been careful
to get a room with a window facing on the square. The
square was La Plaza de la Republica, a small park surrounding the Palace of Justice. Parades with Fidel at
their head made their way up a broad avenue to that
plaza. Then Fidel would speak, orating wildly and
magnificently from the steps of the palace. From his
window Garrison could see those steps.

With the rifle properly mounted on the window
ledge, he could place a bullet in Fidel's open mouth.

He drew the window shade and returned to the
bed. Maybe he wouldn't even have to use the gun, he
thought. Maybe one of the four idiots—Turner or
Hines or Garth or Fenton, wherever the hell they all
were—would save him the trouble. He was in no hurry.
If one of the others killed Fidel, that was fine. He got
his twenty grand just the same, with no risk and no
work. If not, then he set up the gun and squeezed the
trigger. The rifle would be dismantled and tucked away
in the room before Fidel knew he was dead. The Beretta
could stay where it was, in the television set. And he
would be on the next boat to the mainland.

There was a knock on the door. He sighed, raised himself on one elbow. "Who is it?"

"Estrella. Let me in, 'arper."

The name on his identification papers was John Harper, a simple enough name which happened to begin with the one letter Estrella couldn't manage. He stood up, wrapped a bath towel around his middle and opened the door for her. She came inside.

She was very young and very beautiful. She had a tiny waist, solid breasts and hips, a red rosebud of a mouth and deep brown eyes that a man could get lost in. She was a prostitute; Garrison had managed to pick her up without trying very hard one night in the hotel's bar. Now she came to his room every evening. Sometimes she would tell him that she was in love with him. Other times she would not say a word, would simply make love with him in fiery silence.

Now she ran a soft hand over his chest. "You take a bath," she said. "All you Yankees, every minute you take another bath. You take too many baths, 'arper."

"And you don't take enough."

She pouted. "You don't like how I smell?"

His hands cupped her taut buttocks, drew her close. She was a full head shorter than he was. He lowered his face and inhaled the sweet animal fragrance that rose between her breasts.

"I like how you smell," he said. "You smell of sex. You smell like you want to get into bed."

"And you? You don' wan'?"

"I wan', Estrella."

"You make fun how I talk. Don' I talk awright?"

"You talk like a magpie. Come here, Estrella."

She came into his arms again and he held her close. She wore a thin white cotton dress with nothing under it. He could feel the heat of her body through the thin cloth. She squirmed against him, and her hands found the towel around his waist.

"You don' need that towel, 'arper."

"You're right."

"So," she said. The towel dropped to the floor and she stepped back, looked at him, grinned. "You're naked," she said. "I love you, 'arper. I love you, you bastard."

He reached for her, caught her. She squealed with delight as he lifted her into the air and dumped her down on the bed. Then he was on the bed beside her, his hands busy with the white cotton dress. She laughed and giggled, pushed his hands away playfully. He grabbed her and kissed her. His tongue went between her lips and suddenly she moaned out loud; all the playfulness turned instantly to passion now and she was urging her body against his, kissing hard, holding tight.

They took her dress off. His hands went over her body, stroking the silken luxury of perfect skin, rubbing the slightly rounded stomach, cupping full breasts taut with womanliness, then kissing the upthrust nipples while she writhed wantonly on the bed. She said *'arper, 'arper, 'arper,* repeated again and again a name that was not really his.

There was no element of time, no sense of space. Reality was suspended momentarily; rather, reality consisted only of Garrison and the girl, only of the meeting of bodies. There was one instant of irony when he realized again that they were making love on top of a high-powered rifle, but the thought was submerged by a wave of passion.

Then he was on his back looking at the ceiling without seeing it, waiting for his heartbeat to return to normal. He breathed deeply, closed his eyes, opened them again. He turned and saw her beside him, her eyes watching him. She looked like a cat by the fireplace, like an infant in the fetal posture. She looked beautiful.

" 'arper," she said, her sleek, naked body arching toward him.

"Mmmmm?"

"When you go back to America?"

"Not tonight. I'll be busy tonight."

"Don't kid aroun'. When you go back?"

"I don't know. Not for a while."

"When you go," she said softly, "you take me with you. No?"

"No."

"Why not?"

Because I'm a killer, he thought. *Hired killers don't*

carry pretty little whores in their suitcases. They travel light.

" 'arper? You married, 'arper?"

It was a convenient lie but he passed it up, shaking his head.

"Then why not take me with you? I love you, 'arper. An' you love me. I get in your blood."

"And I get in your—"

"Don't talk dirty. Why not, 'arper?"

"I'm sleepy," he said. "Stay here tonight. We'll talk about it in the morning. Right now I want to go to sleep."

"You wan' me to stay tonight?"

"Yeah."

"An' when you leave Cuba, you take me with you?"

"Maybe," he said. "We'll see."

That seemed to satisfy her. He watched her close her eyes and drift off to sleep almost at once, like the contented little animal she was. He did not fall asleep that quickly. He rolled over onto his side, found a pack of cigarettes, smoked one in the near-darkness. He watched the tip of the cigarette glow with life when he drew on it. When he had finished, he stubbed it out in the ashtray on the bedside table, and closed his eyes again. But sleep didn't come.

Take her back to the States? That was a cute idea now, wasn't it? Jesus, he thought, she's just another little piece and Havana is full of a million sluts just like her. And they would all tell you how much they loved

you. So he should bring this one home with him? Like
a war bride, he thought. A goddamned war bride.

Just another little piece, maybe a little better than
most of them, but still nothing special. So why didn't
he hand her her walking papers and get rid of her before she got in his way? Why not?

And it was the damnedest thing. He didn't like her
calling him 'arper. He wished she would call him *Ray*.

A dry, hot, lazy afternoon. Maria sat by the ashes of the
dead campfire. She was cleaning her Sten gun. Only a
fool let his gun become dirty. Once she had seen such
a fool with a dirty gun. A troup of Castro's forces had
attacked, and one of their men fired his weapon. And
it had blown up in his face, had disintegrated it.

She went on cleaning her gun, humming softly to
herself. Her mind was busy with thought and she did
not hear Garth until he was at her side.

Then she whirled. This big man frightened her;
twice already he had put his hands on her, bothering
her.

"You be nice to me," he said now. "You be nice and
we'll have a good time."

She did not understand the words; they were in
English and she didn't know the language. But the
meaning was clear enough even though the words were
unintelligible. He wanted her.

She tried to get to her feet. But he put his big hands
on her shoulders and pushed. She fell down and he

threw himself down beside her. She could smell the strong animal smell of his sweat. He was no man, this Garth. He was a pig.

She cursed him in Spanish and he smiled, not understanding her words. He reached out a massive paw that closed around her breast. He squeezed and she writhed in terror. He was hurting her.

"You and me," he said. "We'll have ourselves a ball."

He was lying on top of her now, his breath strong in her face. She felt one of his hands forcing itself between her thighs, touching her. She twisted, got a hand free, slapped at his face. He only leered at her.

She saw the heat building within him, noticed the way he was breathing faster. She lay there, fighting him, waiting for the rape to begin, knowing he was stronger and she could not resist him. His hands were busy with her full, firm breasts, busy with her groin. She would have screamed but there was no one to hear.

He might have raped her, but he did not. There were sounds of men coming, sounds of the rest of the party returning to the camp. He stopped, listened, grunted.

"We got company," he said. "Sometime soon, honey. We'll have to get this finished, you and me."

"I will kill you," she told him in Spanish. "I will kill you. I will shoot you and watch you die."

*

That night she spoke to Manuel. In Spanish, Maria said: "That Garth continues to bother me. Today he put his hands on me. Several times."

"You have no man," Manuel said. "He wishes to be the one."

"I don't want a man."

"It is not natural," Manuel said. "A woman without a man."

"I do not want one. And even if I did, it would not be Garth."

Manuel shrugged expressively. "If you took another man, perhaps Garth would cease to bother you."

"I cannot. Not any man. You know what happened."

What happened was simple. Four months ago Maria had had a man, a husband. She and her man fought in the hills with Manuel. Then one day the Castristas caught them both on patrol. There were four of the Castristas. First they killed Maria's husband by shooting him in the head with a machine gun until he had no head left. That was a picture which never left Maria's mind, the picture of Carlos lying on his back in the dirt with his body ending at the neck, with blood everywhere.

And then she had been raped. The four of them took her in turn, and it didn't do her any good to struggle, but she struggled nevertheless. She kneed one soldier in the groin and tried to gouge the eyes of another. To punish her for this, the four of them burned her breasts with a cigar after they had finished with her. They did not kill her. They left her on the road, living but in fearful pain, as an example to the others. And for dramatic effect they placed Carlos' dead body upon her and tied the two of them together.

Her breasts still bore scars from the cigar burning. And she wanted no man now, no man at all.

"If this Garth bothers me," she said levelly, "I will kill him."

"This would be unfortunate. He is a good fighter."

"He is stupid."

"That is true," Manuel said. "But he is fearless and strong. He helps us. And he will help with the ambush, when Castro rides his Jeep through the valley of death. He will be helpful. It would be good if you did not kill Garth."

"If he bothers me—"

"After Castro is dead," Manuel said, "then you may kill Garth. I will help you."

"You could tell him to stay away from me."

"I have told him this."

"And it does no good?"

"He is not a man who thinks," Manuel said slowly. "He is a man who decides, and who acts. One cannot reason with him."

Maria looked away. It was night; the rest of the band slept. The moon was high overhead, a thin crescent.

"We must kill Castro soon," she said.

"I have heard reports. They say he will travel to Santiago one week from Sunday. He will come on the road from Bayamo and Palma Soriano, of course. We may have the ambush between Palma and Santiago."

"There will be patrols."

"Many patrols, many guards. It is a chance."

Maria nodded thoughtfully. "We must kill him soon," she said. "Because very soon I shall kill this Garth. I shall shoot him and watch him die."

Turner stretched, stood up. He took his pack of cigarettes from the nightstand and put them into his shirt pocket. They were Cuban cigarettes which Señora Luchar had given him. He had discovered that he preferred them to American cigarettes.

"I'm going out," he told Hines.

"You kidding?"

"No. Why should I be kidding? Because I might get picked up by cops? To hell with that."

"Well, you might."

Turner was shaking his head. "Uh-uh," he said. "Look, I know the fugitive routine. I went all over the States with the police looking for me. I got used to looking over my shoulder every time I took a leak. I don't have to do that here. Nobody's on my tail."

"I still think you're taking a chance."

"Then you still don't get it. Hell, you don't know what it's like to be hunted. It's like nothing in the world. You don't relax. I told you about what happened, didn't I? About the girl and the pig with her?"

"You told me."

"Yeah. Afterward I got drunk and slept it off. Then I woke up and remembered. Since then I never relaxed, not once. I kept running and I kept hiding and I kept looking over my shoulder. It's quite a feeling. Not a good feeling."

Hines didn't say anything.

"Now we're in Cuba. And it's a hell of a thing, Jim. Nobody's looking for me now. If I went out in the streets and told the world I killed a whore and her customer in Charleston they wouldn't give a damn. I'm a free man. I don't have to spend my time in a stinking basement. I can get out in the open air."

"I hope you're right."

"I'll chance it," he said. "Take it easy."

Hines stayed on the edge of his bunk. He picked up an American magazine that the Luchar woman had brought, leafed through it absently. He tossed it onto the bed and wandered over to the heavy wooden work bench. It was like the one his old man had in the cellar. The old man used to like to make things. They were always things that he could have bought for half the price it cost him to make them himself, and they always came out a little wrong, but his old man got a kick out of it.

His old man had never made bombs. And that was what they were making now. Impact bombs with a power charge of TNT that would go off on contact. You took the bomb, gave it a heave, and when it landed it went off like…well, like a bomb. What else?

He didn't know a hell of a lot about bombs. Neither did Turner, really, but Turner at least knew what was supposed to go into the thing and how it all worked. He had put together a list of materials for Señora Luchar, metal casing for the exterior, TNT for the charge, various other gimmicks and gizmos that ought to work. And Turner had done most of the work, drilling and sawing and fitting the casing, figuring out the right charge. Now they had two bombs almost completed. All that was needed was a few finishing touches and a strong heave in the right direction. And that would be that.

He wondered who the bomb would kill. Besides Castro, of course. God alone knew how much of a bomb they had. It could turn out to be the world's greatest dud since Primo Carnera or it could blow half of Havana off the map, for all they could tell. They might get Fidel Castro. They might also get some of his soldiers, and some other politicians. And some people in the crowds, some women and children, some—

Hell. This wasn't a game. He had a score to settle, had a slate to wipe clean. Joe was dead, damn it to hell, and Castro was going to get his, and if some poor clowns got in the way it was their tough luck. It was part of the game.

Like revolutionary justice?

Well, now.

He left the room. He was thinking too damned much

and it was just getting him jumpy. Maybe Turner had the right idea—take it easy, do your job, keep your mouth shut, and go out in the streets and enjoy the sights. No thanks, he thought. Not yet. I'll stay indoors right now, thank you.

He took a flight of stairs two at a time, walked through the kitchen to the living room. The Luchar dame was sitting in an easy chair reading a Cuban newspaper. She looked up at him.

"Your friend Turner went out," she said. "How come you decided to stick around?"

"I don't know."

"Sit down," she said. "Want coffee? Or maybe some lunch?"

He told her that sounded fine. She got up and he watched her leave the room. She spoke English with an American accent and this got him, got him good. It didn't fit with the rest of her. Christ, she was straight out of *A Tale of Two Cities*, a twentieth-century Madame Defarge who didn't know how to knit. She got to him, sometimes. Gave him the chills. He wasn't sure why, but that was the way it worked.

She came back with a plate of *arroz con pollo* and a cup of steaming coffee. The chicken-and-rice dish was spicy, tasty. He hadn't realized how hungry he was.

"Have you been back in Cuba long?" he asked her.

"Since the revolution won. Batista left and I came back. Why?"

"I just wondered," he said. "Maybe you knew my brother."

"He was here?"

He nodded. "His name was Joe," he said. "Joe Hines." She looked thoughtful.

"You remember him?"

"I remember," she said. "I didn't know him, not person to person. I knew who he was, of course. Castro had him shot."

He nodded bitterly.

"Of course," she said. "I wondered why you were here. Revenge, the rest of it. Am I right?"

"Of course."

"I see," she said. She turned away slightly. "Well, one must have reasons. And the reasons matter only to the individual. It doesn't make a bit of difference why you are here, only what you do here. The results are more important than the reasons."

"I don't get it."

"Don't you?"

"No," he said, annoyed. "You use a lot of words but you don't say a hell of a lot. What are you getting at?"

She smiled shallowly. "I told you. It does not matter."

"It matters to me."

She shrugged. "More *arroz con pollo?* There's a whole pot of it on the stove."

"No, thanks—"

"More coffee?"

"No," he said. "Look, you're trying to change the subject. I don't want it changed."

"Sometimes it's a good idea."

"Damn it!" He stood up, his hands balled into fists of tension at his sides. "Look, you've got something that you're not telling me and I just don't get it. I want to hear what it's all about before I crack up. If you've got something to say, say it. Otherwise quit playing games with me!"

She smiled again, unnervingly. "So young," she said. "When a man is so young everything is simple, true? Easy questions and easy answers. I wish I had learned how to lie to my friends. It is easy to lie to enemies. I cannot lie to friends."

"What's that supposed to mean?"

"Only that your brother was a traitor."

He stared at her. She was crazy, that was all. She was some kind of a nut and he was wasting his time paying attention to her. She was out of her skull, off her rocker. She was batty.

"I am speaking the truth, Hines. But you don't have to believe me if you don't want to. Perhaps you shouldn't believe me."

"A traitor to Castro," he said desperately. "He saw that Castro was ruining the country so he broke with him. That's what you mean, isn't it? He broke with Castro so Castro called him a traitor and had him shot. That's it, huh? He was a traitor the same way you're a traitor, because he wanted what was best for Cuba and—"

"No."

The single syllable stopped him. He broke off, stared, lowered his eyes. For a long moment he stood looking at his shoes. Señora Luchar was still sitting in the easy chair, her eyes quiet. He sat down himself, with a great heaviness and looked at her.

"You'd better tell me all of it."

"Would it serve a purpose?"

"Yes."

"Don't be an ass," she said. "Don't be a damn fool. Castro killed your brother and blood is thicker than principles. You still have to get your revenge. Joe Hines was still your brother and you still have to get revenge on the man who killed him. Why knock yourself out?"

"Tell me."

"Listen—"

"Tell me!"

She sighed. "Your brother was a hero," she said easily. "In the beginning in Oriente, he was a bearded hero with the rest of them. He fought like a hero and he laughed like a hero. And, with the rest of those bearded ones, he won. He marched into Havana with a gun on his belt and a gleam in his eye. He won, Hines."

"I know all that."

"But you don't know the rest. He had his own ideas, your brother did. He saw riches all around, saw a whole nation which could be of use to him. He had these visions. He saw himself at the top of it all, running the country, with a host of grateful Cubans kissing his rump and telling him he was God. He fought with us, Hines, but he was not of us. He was an Anglo and wanted to take up that white man's burden you all carry so selflessly. He wanted a batch of inferior Cubans smiling up at him and kissing his rump."

"He wasn't like that."

"He became like that. He and two others organized a movement. A counter-revolutionary movement. They were not going to push out Castro because Castro was undemocratic. They were going to replace him because they wanted to have his power."

Hines said nothing. He was numb.

"So Castro had him shot. And he deserved it, Hines. Your brother was no good. He started as a hero and ended as a traitor. Still, your revenge must be carried out. Blood is thicker than principles."

"Joe—"

"Was a traitor."

His eyes suddenly went wild and he sprang to his feet. "Damn you!" he shouted. "Do you think I'm going to believe something like that? Joe was my brother, you dried up bitch! He was a wonderful guy. He was a hero. He did wonderful things for your crummy country and you just want to look for rotten things to say about him. You—"

"Believe what you wish," she said softly.

"What I wish? You think what I *wish* has a damn thing to do with it? I believe what I've got to believe, damn it. You can go to hell!"

She did not say a word. He stormed past her, pounded down the stairs to the basement room. He slammed a door, swung his fist against the wall, blinked his eyes at the pain. He walked to the bed, threw himself down on it, then stood up again. He punched his pillow, punched the wall again with his other hand, and sat once more on the bed.

Joe, he thought. *Joe, where are you? Tell me about it, Joe. Tell me she's a lying bitch. Tell me she's handing me a load of crap. Please, Joe. I need you, Joe.*

I miss you, Joe.

He stood up, sat down, stood up, sat down again. He clenched and unclenched his hands, trying first to accept what the woman had told him, then trying not to believe it, torn constantly back and forth, torn in half.

He wanted to cry but he did not know how.

six

To All Who May Be Concerned

By this means it is announced that any person who furnishes information leading to a successful operation against any rebel nucleus commanded by Fidel Castro, Raul Castro, Crescencio Perez, Guillermo Gonzalez, or any other leader, will be rewarded in accordance with the importance of the information, with the understanding that it will never be less than $5,000. This reward will vary from $5,000 to $100,000, the highest amount, that is, $100,000, being payable for the head of Fidel Castro.

Note: The name of the informer shall never be revealed.

This notice appeared throughout Cuba. It was posted in every section of Oriente Province, tacked to tree upon tree, nailed to fence post after fence post. Batista was growing desperate; the head of Fidel Castro was now easily worth one hundred thousand dollars to him. Castro had returned to Cuba. He headed a tiny rebel band which grew in numbers every day, a band which caused the throne of the dictator to tremble.

The Gramma *was a yacht owned by an American named Erickson who lived in Mexico City. In early 1956 Colonel Alberto Bayo had begun training Castro's troops on a Mexican ranch, leading them in forced marches, instructing them in combat techniques, guerrilla warfare, compressing into a three-month period all the training they would have received in three years at a military academy. By November of '56 Castro was ready. Comrades bought the* Gramma *from Erickson and Castro filled the ship with his eighty-two soldiers and all the arms at their disposal. The loading was conducted in secret at Tuxpan, a river port in Vera Cruz. On November 25th the ship set sail, cruising down the Rio Tuxpan to the Gulf of Mexico, heading eastward for Oriente Province and war with Batista.*

While Castro was at sea, underground forces launched an uprising in Santiago. Batista replied by suspending all civil rights in the eastern sectors of the island, sending tank battalions to Oriente to crush the rebellion. Castro was sailing into the mouth of hell. Batista knew he was coming, knew the revolt he planned. Yet the Gramma *landed on December 2 and Castro's forces disappeared into the hills.*

The revolution was in progress.

It was a new sort of revolution. The first order of business was that of survival, an impossible enough task at the beginning. The government troops were everywhere, rooting out rebels and crushing them by sheer weight of numbers. Of Castro's original landing party of eighty-two men, only twenty-two managed to stay alive. And ten of those were captured, leaving a band of twelve to carry on the revolution in the hills. Could twelve men topple a tyrant? It seemed to be a question not worth answering, a thorough impossibility.

But Batista was afraid, and had good reason to be. His answer was terror and repression, terror which had to be witnessed to be believed. His air force crossed the hills of Oriente time and time again, strafing fields at random on the off chance that rebels lay hiding there. His soldiers roamed Oriente, arresting peasants at will on charges of aiding Castro. Men and women were murdered. Peasants were tortured by the score in an attempt to gain information about Castro.

Terror was a poor weapon. Peasants who had given no thought to politics now saw Castro's men on one side, brave and honest, paying for food and shelter. And on the other side were Batista's mercenaries, taking what they wanted, looting, raping and slaughtering. These peasants listened to Castro's promises of agrarian reform, heard him speak of liberty and freedom. The twelve ragged rebels grew in number. New recruits swelled their ranks, and peasants throughout Oriente were ready to feed and hide them from the government soldiers.

The spirit of rebellion which Castro had started in

the hills soon spread to the cities. Underground cells sprang into being, harassing Batista's men and gathering ammunition and supplies for the rebels in the east. A band of Havana students fearlessly attempted to assassinate Batista; the plot misfired and the assassins were machine-gunned outside the palace. The dictator grew increasingly desperate. His secret police made midnight arrests, and citizens vanished into jails and died there. Libertarian newspapers were suspended from publication. Their editors were tortured, murdered.

Castro could not be crushed. His men put the full techniques of guerrilla warfare into operation, striking, running and living to strike again. They sucked raw sugar cane to stay alive. They threw away their razors, vowing to remain unshaven until the revolution was a reality. The full beard became the emblem of liberty, and the public saw the barbudos—*the bearded ones— as a new generation of freedom fighters, a race of supermen.*

Batista's wave of terror could not defeat Fidel Castro. The healthy revolution feeds on terror, thrives on it. Every act of repression wins support for the men who are fighting to overthrow the oppressor. Still, the terror of the dictator served a purpose.

It did not defeat Castro. But it began to change him.

It is not easy to fight a clean fight against an opponent who fights dirty. It is no simple matter to observe the Marquess of Queensberry rules in a contest with one who is trying to gouge your eyes and plant a knee in your groin. The temptation is always present to fight fire with fire, to greet terror with new terror.

Castro did this. There is still the question whether he ever intended to fight any other way. After all, many of his followers had been Communists for some time. Many of them had spent time in Russia and had learned Communist tactics there.

At the Sierra Maestro, Castro found a ranch foreman who had accused tenant farmers of being pro-rebel and who had greatly increased his personal land holdings at their expense. Castro's men seized the foreman, tried him, and executed him.

This was revolutionary justice.

Revolutionary justice. *It was a fresh term, a new term, a carefully chosen rationalization for fighting fire with fire, for meeting the terror of Batista with the terror of the rebels. If Batista could torture and kill those who aided rebels, then Castro could leave the mutilated bodies of Batistianos as a grim souvenir of his purpose. If Batista could burn houses and slaughter peasants, Castro could go him one better and set sugarcane fields afire and lay waste to thousands of acres of farmland.*

If Batista could retreat into paranoia, seeing enemies on every side and leveling vengeful cries in every direction, Castro could adopt this paranoia and im-

prove upon it. He, too, could reward those who followed him. And he, too, could swear eternal vengeance upon his enemies.

His movement was gaining ground; the ultimate success of his revolution was inevitable. But he himself was changing. Either that or he had been carefully hiding his real purpose all along.

seven

The highway runs from Manzanillo, on the Gulf of Guacanayabo, almost due east to Santiago. Its course is roughly parallel to the southern coasts of Oriente Province, passing through the towns of Bayamo and Jiguani and Palma Soriano before reaching the end of the line. It is a broad, two-lane highway, paved with blacktop but maintained poorly. There are potholes here and there, the asphalt blacktop eroded or gouged out, and an automobile's tires can take a beating on the road.

The land on either side of the road is rough and hilly. The soil is fertile and the rain plentiful, but this particular area is not good for the raising of sugar cane, the crop that is for Cuba what cotton was for the ante-bellum Southern United States. A little tobacco is grown here and there along the highway. Mostly, the land is given over to small truck-farms, or is abandoned to nature. There are hills, there are valleys, there are dense growths of shrubbery and brush.

There are also rebels.

It was late afternoon. Matt Garth lay flat on his back upon a threadbare army blanket and listened to the train. The train ran a zigzag course from Manzanillo to

Glorieta in the east, bypassing Santiago. The train was now perhaps a mile from them, but it could be heard easily through the still air. It was the only sound audible.

Garth yawned and scratched himself. The spics were out somewhere, he thought. Out chasing fleas or something, for God's sake. He didn't know how in hell they did it, but every afternoon they went skulking off into the woods, and every night they came back with something to eat—a sack of beans, a pot of rice, a chicken with its neck twisted, a few eggs, once even a young pig taken too soon from its mother. Garth wasn't too clear on how they managed it, whether they copped the food from farmers who were on their side or whether they just stole it. He didn't much care.

He lit a cigarette, took two puffs on it and put it out. He was going crazy, that was the trouble. He was going off his nut, roaming around in the goddamned mountains and eating rice and beans three times a day and waiting for something to happen. The fighting wasn't bad but they hadn't had any of that in too long, not since they cooked the six soldiers in the Jeep. Since then it was plenty of rambling, plenty of sleeping outside, plenty of goddamned beans and rice, and nothing else.

Oh, yeah. Plenty of the broad, that Maria, shaking those big tits and that hot ass right in his face, then pulling it all away the minute he got interested. The tease, the damn tease—she was driving him screwy. A girl who tossed it around like that ought to be ready to give some of it away. It would be a little better if she was at least putting out for somebody else. But not her, not that Maria bitch. She slept alone, slept by her goddamned self, and she stuck her tits in Garth's face every other minute.

She was around now, he knew. She was over by the shore, scrubbing down pots and plates, oiling guns, making herself useful. And Fenton was around too, for all the goddamned good he was. Fenton, the punk, wasn't doing him a hell of a lot of good. Fenton could speak English, all right, but Fenton still didn't talk to him. He just sat around doing nothing all the time, maybe smoking a little, maybe talking to Manuel, the only spic who could speak English. Fenton talked to Manuel more than he talked to Garth, and Manuel never talked to Garth, and Garth couldn't take it. He didn't have leprosy, for God's sake.

His mind started to work. Fenton was sitting by himself, doing nothing. And Maria was there, too. But if Fenton wasn't around, if Fenton wanted to take a walk somewhere, then he would be alone with Maria. She was a tough bitch, tough as nails, but he was a man and he was sure one hell of a lot stronger than she was. So what if she screamed? Nobody would hear her. And what could she do later? Not a hell of a lot, because they needed him for the big play against Castro.

He thought it over for a minute or two. But thinking was a waste of time, thinking only gave him a headache. You could think all day long, the way Fenton did, and what the hell did it get you? Nothing, nothing at all. Thinking was not Garth's kick. He wanted to do something instead. Something that would get that broad on her back with her knees pointing at the sun.

He knew her type, too. All she needed was a man to show her who was boss and then she'd come down off her high horse in no time at all. She needed a man, one who could take charge, and once he showed her what it was all about she wouldn't be cold-shouldering him any more. Hell, by the time he was done with her he'd be beating her off with a club. She'd be after him all the time, he decided.

All he had to do was take her the first time.

So. He stood up, ambled over to Fenton. Fenton was reading a paperback novel, his eyes on the page, a cigarette burning itself to ashes between two of his fingers. Garth cleared his throat and Fenton looked up, his eyes asking a question.

"I was thinking," Garth said. "I was thinking it's a nice day and you maybe should take a walk."

"You want to go someplace?"

"Not me," Garth said. "You."

Fenton said nothing.

"Just a little walk," Garth went on innocently. "A little walk, maybe scout around or something. You wouldn't have to be gone long. Ten, maybe fifteen, even twenty minutes. No more."

"Why?"

Garth shrugged.

Then Fenton got it. "You're making a mistake," he told him, "A big mistake."

"Yeah?"

"Yes. The girl doesn't want you. If you force her we'll all have trouble. Why can't you leave her alone?"

"That's my business, Fenton."

"It's mine as well. You'll get twenty thousand dollars, Garth. You can have all the women in the world with that much money. Can't you leave this one alone until then?"

"What's the matter? Got the hots for her yourself?"

"No."

"I bet that's it," Garth said. "Why, you little dried-up old fart! You want the broad yourself, don't you?"

"No. Leave her alone, Garth. You'll ruin everything. You'll—"

But Garth didn't hear any more of it, mainly because that was all Fenton had a chance to say. Garth's mind worked simply but efficiently. He had managed to dope out the fact that Fenton wasn't going to go for a walk, and that if Fenton stayed around he would only make trouble. So Garth did the simplest thing possible under that set of circumstances. He hit Fenton once, on the side of the head.

Once was enough. The blow was a measured chop, hard enough to knock a man out, hard enough to keep him out for ten or fifteen minutes. Which would be plenty of time.

Time for the broad.

He found her at the edge of the stream, sitting cross-legged in the shade of a huge matto grosso palm, dressed as always in the army field jacket and the khaki pants. Her eyes came up slowly, meeting his, finding something frightening there that caused them to widen in terror. He met her fearful expression with a smile that came out lecherous and evil.

"It's about time," he said. And he stepped toward her.

She understood the meaning if not the words. She had been scrubbing a cast iron skillet, and as he moved at her she threw the skillet at him, aiming for his face. He brushed it aside with one hand, then moved to kick aside the Sten gun she was reaching for. She started to scramble to her feet but he slapped her hard on the side of her face and she fell down again.

"Now," he said.

He fell on her, roughly, savage and blind with his hunger. She fought him, her nails driving for his face, for his eyes, but he pinned her hands behind her back and tore the field jacket open. Beneath it she wore only a white T-shirt, no brassiere. He ripped the T-shirt from her body. Her breasts were enticing mounds of golden flesh, the tips dark and taut, and he filled his hands with them, squeezing her, hurting her.

There was terror in her eyes now, terror mingling with fear, hatred, loathing and anger. He ignored all this. He was impatient, a stallion aching to mount a mare. He tore at her pants, at the damned khaki pants she always wore. He got them down over her hips, over her thighs, down to her knees. Her underpants were wispy white nylon and he shredded them.

"Don't fight," he said, not caring that she could not understand him. "Don't fight, don't give me a hard time. Just relax and enjoy it. It won't be so bad, you little bitch. Just relax. You might like it."

But she fought. One knee tried for his groin but he swerved his body and blocked the blow with his hips. One hand got loose, went for his throat, but he caught the hand and bent it back against her wrist until she moaned with pain. The knee tried again, and this time he lost patience, burying a hamlike fist in the softness of her flat stomach so that she doubled up in agony and made a sound like a man when you shot him in the guts with a small-caliber pistol.

He hit her again, in the same spot, and the fight sagged out of her like air from a punctured tire. He struggled with his own clothing now, opened his pants, readied himself.

There was a gunshot. A bullet passed far over Garth's head. Garth froze, waiting.

Then a voice. Fenton's. Harsh, cold, crisp, unafraid.

"Get up, Garth. Get up, you pig, or I'll shoot you where you are. I'll kill you, Garth."

There was no room for doubt in the tone of the little man's voice. It was not easy for Garth to get up.

He was primed, ready, and it was not at all easy to give up now when the prize was there on the ground ready to be taken.

He got up.

"Button your pants. Then get the hell away from her, Garth, and stay away from her. Because if you go near her again I'll kill you. You're an animal, Garth. Get away from her and leave her alone."

Garth walked away, ashamed and bitter. He hated Fenton and he hated the girl and he loathed himself with a flat, dull loathing. He had had her there and he had not taken her. That rat Fenton had fouled things up, that rat bastard.

He went back to his blanket and found his cigarettes.

The café was on Calle de las Mujeres Bonitas, the street of the pretty women. There were no pretty women around, none that Turner could see. But he was not anxious to meet any, not just now. Now all he wanted to do was sit where he was sitting, sip the glass of good red wine he had at hand, and talk with Ernesto.

Ernesto was a thick-set Cuban with a walrus mustache and sleepy eyes, a man's man who talked easily, swore freely, drank heavily and, if he was to be believed, fornicated incessantly. Turner had met him there, at the café, two days ago. Turner had bought him a glass of wine. Then Ernesto had returned the favor. They took a table together and talked.

They were talking now.

"It seems to me that you have no problem," Ernesto was saying in Spanish. "You have killed a whore and her lover, true? And so the North American police would hang you."

"They take a dim view of murder."

"So," Ernesto said. "In North America, there you have a problem. But here, in Cuba? No problem, no problem at all."

"What about extradition?" Turner asked. He knew the States had an extradition treaty with Cuba; they had one with every Latin American country, even with Brazil now. But in Brazil there were loopholes. You could marry a local girl and immunize yourself from extradition. Or you could get to the right official with enough money.

"There is a treaty," Ernesto allowed.

"So I have a problem—"

"No. In the old days, in the days before the revolution, then you would have had a problem. But these days things are not so good between Señor Castro and your government, true? Your government says that a man named Turner is a criminal, a murderer. And our Señor Castro laughs, because he knows that this Turner has killed no one in Cuba. So there will be no extradition. You have broken no laws here and you may remain here."

It was something Turner had thought of before. Cuba was as good as Brazil and as safe. But there was still the matter of twenty thousand dollars.

"I would need money," Turner said. "Where would I work?"

Ernesto shrugged magnificently. "Why work? *I* do not work. It is not necessary to work."

"But I have no money."

"Ah," Ernesto said. "It is not difficult to get money. One buys, one sells. One acts as an agent in such transactions. One lives cleverly, making oneself useful to others. Look at me, my friend. Before the revolution, I worked for a man named Antonio Torelli. Señor Torelli was a gangster from New York, a man who owned a casino here in Havana. A very important man. I worked at his casino. I was a dealer, a croupier. Señor Torelli also bought a bordello, also in Havana. I managed this house for him, kept the girls on their toes. I earned good money for this work."

"And?"

"And there was a revolution. So. All at once Señor Torelli is on a plane to Florida and I no longer have a job. The casinos run by American gangsters are closed. The bordellos run by American gangsters are also closed. Have I starved?"

"It would take you years to starve," Turner said.

Ernesto looked at his own girth and laughed. "You jest," he said. "But it is true. When one is clever, when one thinks with one's brain, it takes a long time to starve. It takes eternity."

Turner finished his wine. He noticed that Ernesto's glass was also empty and signaled to the dark-skinned waiter. The man came over and filled both glasses to the brim. Turner paid. Ernesto nodded his thanks. They touched glasses with ceremony and sipped the wine.

"You would not starve here, my friend, and you would have money. I am a man who has many deals working, many vistas of opportunity. You could perhaps become a partner."

Turner smiled. "In crime?"

"A harsh word. There are many men who have more money than they need, and less brains than they ought to possess. One can relieve men of money. Or, if you have scruples, there is always work. You understand construction?"

"I've been on crews."

"Men are needed," Ernesto said. "Men who can run heavy equipment, men of that nature. Few men in Cuba understand such machines. The pay is high."

Turner sipped more wine, thinking it over. Either way, he could make a living in Cuba. Either way.

"You said that you have no money. True?"

"True."

"But what will you do for money in Brazil? It is no more easy to live there without money."

But I'll have money then, he thought. *I'll become a criminal again, a murderer again, by killing Castro. And I'll run again, and I'll pick up my twenty grand in blood money and hightail it to Brazil. And after a while maybe I'll even learn how to relax again. How to live*

*and enjoy life without looking over my shoulder for
the law.*

"I pry too much," Ernesto was saying now. "I ask perhaps too many questions, and this is not the role of a
friend. And I am your friend, Turner, and you are my
friend. True?"

"True."

"So. Let us finish our wine and go to the bordello. I
shall pay, if you will permit me. Today—this morning—
three of your countrymen came to me. Young boys,
students in one of your colleges. They wished to pur-
chase some marijuana cigarettes."

"And you sold them some?"

Ernesto frowned sadly. "Of course not. Young, pink-
faced boys—the marijuana would have them walking
across the sky, skipping like lambs from cloud to cloud.
I told them to wait for me. I went to my garden and
harvested weeds—plantain, grasses. I dried these in
my oven and added catnip. I rolled a huge quantity of
cigarettes. These I sold to your countrymen for a fine
sum of money. And there is no danger, because they
may smoke them forever without being affected."

Turner laughed.

"So I shall pay," Ernesto continued. "The girls at
this house are a delight, my friend. Young and clever.
There is one girl I think you shall like. A Chinese. Her
father was Chinese, her mother Cuban. A lovely girl."

They finished the wine and walked to a hotel several blocks away. In the lobby Ernesto talked volubly

to the madam, a fat Cuban woman with pendulous breasts. Two girls came out—the Oriental Ernesto had spoken of and a young Cuban girl with dyed blond hair. Ernesto went off with the blonde and Turner followed the Chinese girl to her room.

She had tiny hands and feet, delicate features. She spoke Spanish with a Chinese accent. She kissed like a child and made love like a woman. Her skin was soft, her body firm.

She stood still, her hands over her head, while Turner removed her clothing. His hands moved over her silky skin, fondling her beautifully resilient breasts, fascinated by their tautness, his tongue circling the dark, saucy nipples. Then she made him stay still while she took off his clothing. She touched his naked body, stroked him in new and delicious ways that aroused him subtly and undeniably.

He took her in his arms, and they went to the bed.

They were on the bed for a long time before they made love. The girl was an artist with the caress, the kiss. Her hands were everywhere, her lips active, her seeking tongue industrious. She set Turner on fire. He kissed her firm little breasts again, squeezed the ripe globes of her buttocks and stroked her inner thighs, making her leap with anticipation.

Then they made love. It was warm, intense, demanding. She was anxious to please. Turner felt like a master, a god, a man.

Afterward, he and Ernesto walked through the

streets of downtown Havana, stopped for a glass of beer here and there, smoked Cuban cigars and relaxed in the soft warmth of Havana at night.

"And you wish to leave this?" Ernesto demanded. "This ease, this blissful atmosphere? This for Brazil?"

"I enjoy Havana," Turner admitted.

"Of course you do. You will stay."

"Perhaps."

"You will go to the government," Ernesto said, "and you will tell them that in the United States you killed a man and a woman, and that you stole into Cuba illegally. They will permit you to stay. They will assist you."

And Turner started to laugh. The irony of it was magnificent—he would be asking for help from the man he proposed to kill!

"Good food and good drinks," the businessman said. "And good little women, best in the world. But I'm getting out of here, Harper. I'll tell you, give me the States any time. You can relax there. They appreciate business, don't try to push a man out once he gets where he belongs. Here it doesn't work that way."

Garrison looked at him. The man was fat and he perspired easily. He had said that his name was Burley, Lester Burley—call me Les. Garrison neither liked nor disliked him. They were in the bar at the Nacional and they were drinking. Soon Garrison would go upstairs, and then Estrella would join him for the evening. He didn't mind putting up with call-me-Les Burley until then.

"You're in business here, Burley?"

"Les," Burley corrected. "Yes, I'm in business here. Nothing fancy, import and export, actually. Mostly cigars, buying tobaccos and selling them to a few cigar makers in Tampa. Ever been to Tampa?"

"No," Garrison said.

"You'd like it—good town. Couple factories there— Havana Royale, Garcia Supreme—I sell 'em a lot of their stuff. Handle it, you might say. You're in real estate, Harper?"

Garrison nodded.

"Meaning you buy and you sell?"

"That's right."

"This trip business or pleasure?"

"A little of both," Garrison drawled, slipping into his role. "Pleasure before business, I always say. Sort of a motto of mine. But if a chance comes along to make a dollar or two—"

"Up to you, of course," call-me-Les said. "But I wouldn't sign anything, wouldn't put out any cash, wouldn't buy any Cuban real estate. Not if I were you I wouldn't."

"Why?"

"Why?" Burley moistened his lips. "Same reason I'm closing shop and getting the merry hell back to the States. Don't know what I'll get into once I'm back there. Been in Cuba for years and years. More or less have to go into something concerning tobacco, what with my name. You understand?"

Garrison didn't.

"Burley," call-me-Les said. "Burley tobacco. For pipe smoking. Just a coincidence, but a funny one. Don't you think?"

"Oh," Garrison said. "Certainly."

"I'll find something in the States. Not like this country—there a man with drive and know-how still finds opportunities. This place used to be like that. Now they're turning it Socialist, even Communist. And that's why you're a damn fool to pay out good money for a piece of property here. You wouldn't have it long enough to enjoy it. You'd just buy the blame thing and watch them take it away from you."

Garrison nodded thoughtfully. Actually he wasn't paying much attention to Burley. He was thinking about Estrella, remembering the last time they had been together. Now he noticed that Burley was eyeing him, waiting for him to say something.

"You mean confiscations," he said. "I thought they were done with that."

"Not by a long shot. It's just starting. Oh, they took over the big companies already, the oil and the land. Maybe that's enough for Castro. It's beginning to look as though nothing's enough for that boy, but I guess you never know."

"No?"

"Nope. Because he plays ball with the Russians. He gets guns and aid and God-knows-what from them, and that means trouble. I'll betcha he has an idea he'll kinda parlay this whole thing into an empire. You know—commissar of all South America, or something like that."

Burley moistened his lips again. "But he won't last forever. The Commies like him now because they can use him. He's useful, he's handy. But they've got their eye on the whole South American setup and they want it for themselves. And if by some fluke he ever got hold of it, they'd knock him off so fast he wouldn't know what happened to him. He'd find himself on the outside looking in. After that he'd find himself on the inside, looking out." He guffawed at his own joke and then spent the next ten minutes explaining it.

Garrison waited. A slender girl brought drinks and he swallowed half of his. In a few minutes, he thought, it would be time to go to Estrella. She would be better company than this idiot of a cigar salesman who insisted on being called Les. Garrison had had the totally monotonous experience of hearing Burley recount in detail his amatory adventures since age sixteen, and now he was explaining the political picture in Cuba. It was hard for Garrison to decide which was less interesting. Sex was more exciting to him than politics, but at the same time Burley had a way of making any subject a bore.

"You see what I mean, Harper?"

"Sure," Garrison said automatically. "Sure, Les."

"So just you watch. I've got a hunch Castro'll be dead within the next two months. Want to bet on it?"

"No bet. I think you might be right."

Of course he will, Garrison thought. *I'm going to kill him, you poor damned fool. I've got the gun in my room. Want to have a look at it?*

"Here's how it goes, Harper. Castro gets killed—by the Commies, who would rather have their own man in than him. He's bullheaded and overconfident and he can be ordered around only as long as he's getting something out of this Russian deal. Actually, he has no strong convictions. He just likes to run off at the mouth. You know what they used to call him at the university? Loudmouth!

"And you know what the Russians want? To grab Cuba, bump Castro off and then spread a big propaganda blanket saying the U. S. arranged everything and Castro was killed by Americans. Then the whole island goes Communist and we've got one hell of a mess on our hands. Brother, I want to be long gone by then."

"Sure," Garrison said, completely disinterested in Les' predictions, right or wrong. "Well, take care, Les," he said, getting to his feet.

"You got to go?"

"Uh-huh," he said, dropping money to cover the check. "I'll see you."

"Well, at least let me pick up the tab—"

Garrison didn't let him. He left, went to the news-stand in the lobby, picked up a fresh cigar. He took the elevator to his room and let himself in. Everything was as he had left it, and Estrella hadn't shown yet.

He walked to the window, raised the shade, looked out at the plaza where Castro would be speaking. The big public speech was due on July 26th, of course. The anniversary of the movement. And that was the day Castro was going to die, unless one of the other four got to him sooner.

Which seemed doubtful enough.

July 26th was a little less than three weeks away. He laughed; maybe he should have told Burley to revise his figures, should have told him that Castro would be dead in three weeks, not two months. Good old call-me-Les, with his ear pretty damn close to the ground, let me tell you. He would probably drop dead of apoplexy if he knew that John Harper, boy real estate speculator, was the man who was going to put an extra hole in Fidel Castro's head.

Garrison yanked down the window shade, went over to the bed again. The hell with it, he thought. There were plenty of little things to laugh at, things like call-me-Les Burley, but the big things weren't that funny. He had problems of his own.

Estrella was the problem. The easy answer was too easy—get rid of her, forget her, go back to the States and let her rot. That was the right answer but it didn't take care of the problem.

Because the problem was that he *wanted* to take her back with him. She was a new type of woman—she didn't ask for anything, didn't want anything, didn't waste words and didn't get in his hair. She was with him when he wanted her, with him completely and totally. She left him alone when he had to be alone. She knew how to keep her mouth shut.

And he wanted to keep her. That was what it boiled down to—she was a fine little possession and he didn't want to let go of her. And taking her back didn't exactly fit in with his plans, with the pattern of his life. He was going to have to leave in a hurry, a hell of a hurry. He didn't have time to go through war-bride ceremonies. And he might have to lam it hard, might have to bribe some fast-buck pilot to run him home in a hurry. You traveled light in Garrison's business. The first thing you had to learn was not to attach yourself to anything—not to a home, a city, or a thing. You lived out of one suitcase and you were ready to leave that suitcase behind in a jam.

You sure as hell stayed away from love.

Women were fine—they were part of the rewards of the business—expensive, high-flying, one-night gigs. But not love. God in heaven, not love!

A knock at the door.

"Who is it?"

"Estrella. Let me in, 'arper."

He opened the door. She was in his arms, soft and warm. The same excitement was there. It happened every time, the heat, the tension, the desire. Every time.

And afterward:

"I love you, 'arper. I love you."

"I love you, Estrella."

Three days hadn't changed anything. Three days, and as many movements along the road toward Santiago, had done nothing to lift the tension in the rebel band. Garth did not talk to Fenton. Nor did he talk to Manuel, and since no one else spoke English, he, consequently, did not talk to anyone. He spent his time watching Maria. He never went near her, but he never stopped watching her.

And the tension grew. Castro was due within the week. They were in position now, a position they presumably could hold when the time came. Their camp was in the hills, but they were near a rock formation that overlooked the road. From these rocks an ambush would not be difficult at all. Manuel had explained it to Fenton but actually little explanation was necessary.

There were ridges of rock on either side of the road. The road had been cut through and the rock remained around it. Shrubs grew from cracks between boulders to provide additional cover. When the time came, the rebels would station themselves, half on either side of the road. There were ten of them now—Manuel, Maria, Garth, Fenton, Taco Sardo, Francisco Seis, and four new recruits whose names Fenton did not know yet. They would wait for the motor convoy with Castro at its head. Then, as a triumphant Castro sped to Santiago, they would open fire and kill him.

"We may have much luck," Manuel said. "Fidel's brother, Raul, he may be with him. In the car. We may get both birds. Is that how it is said?"

"You mean two birds with one stone."

"That is what I mean. It would be good, killing them both. It would be very good."

Fenton said nothing. He was geared for killing, geared and primed to kill Fidel Castro. It did not occur to him that it would be good or bad to add Fidel's brother to the list of casualties. That did not seem to enter into it.

"Fidel and Raul," Manuel was saying. "I will have much name, *amigo.* I will be the man who executed both the Castros. That will put me very high in the eyes of the people. Is it not so?"

"Of course," Fenton said.

"And I shall have followers. My name will be a unifying force, a force tying Cubans together to rally against the Castro butchers. They may shout my name, *amigo.*"

Fenton nodded uncertainly.

"When Castro is dead," Manuel began. "What will you do then?"

"I don't know," Fenton said honestly. Somehow, he had not given the question any thought. His whole being was geared now to one thing only, the destruction of Castro. What happened after that did not matter. After Castro was dead, Fenton would wait for cancer to kill him. It hardly seemed to matter where he waited, or what he did while he waited. He would be waiting for death.

"You could stay in Cuba."

"Why?"

"With us," Manuel said. "There will be much fighting, of course. A revolution, a full revolution. You have fought with me already, and you could continue to fight with me."

"With you?"

"Of course," Manuel said. He took a knife from his jacket pocket, opened the blade, idly sliced a slender branch from a tree. He began trimming the twigs from the branch.

"I used to make fishing poles in this manner," Manuel said. "When I was a boy."

Fenton kept his mouth shut.

"Here in Cuba," Manuel went on, "there would be a place for you. A better place than in the United States."

"What sort of place?"

Manuel shrugged. Now he was using the knife to peel bark from the branch. He was very deft with the knife. He removed the bark to expose the clean, white wood beneath.

"The other day," Manuel began, "Maria told me what took place."

"You mean with Garth?"

Manuel nodded.

"He knocked me out. I was lucky to come to in time to be much good."

"You were very good," Manuel said. "When I first met you, I thought you were less of a man than you are. I mean that I did not know you would be good at the fighting. I thought you were a quiet man, you know?"

"I am a quiet man."

"You have much heart. I did not know that then. I know it now. Because of what happened with Maria, because of the fighting we have been in together. You have much heart, *amigo*."

Fenton did not know what to say. He was pleased. He felt...alive, useful. He was very pleased.

"Later," Manuel went on. "You will stay with us, yes?"

"If you want me to stay." Why not, he thought. There was no place to go, nothing to do but wait for death. He might as well wait in Cuba. He could die fighting, could die at Manuel's side. Manuel was his friend, his comrade in arms. Better to die at his side than in the teller's cage at the Metropolitan Bank of Lynbrook.

"I want you to stay."

"Then I will stay, Manuel."

Now Manuel was cutting the branch into small sections, then idly tossing the sections into the brush.

"There will be good things for you," he went on, his voice quiet but intense. "When Castro dies, the revolution will begin. And the revolution will take little time. The Castristas will flee the island just as the Batistianos fled before them. And then, *amigo*, Cuba will be ours."

Fenton said nothing. Something was bothering him, gnawing at him. He was unsure what it was.

"Someone will have to lead the nation," Manuel went on. "Someone will have to be the strong man, the ruler."

"Who do you mean?"

Manuel did not answer directly. "A man with reputation," he said easily. "A man the people know. A man, for example, with the scalps of Fidel and Raul at his belt."

"You mean yourself?"

Manuel shrugged. "Someone must take the job. And it would be good to have a man as an assistant. An American, so that the United States will know that Cuba is with the Americans and not the Communists. A man like yourself, for example."

They left it there. But later Fenton thought of the conversation and something like sickness spread through his body. This was the revolution, this was the rising of the people—with Manuel already hungry for power, long before Castro was dead. This was the revolution.

Well, to hell with it. He had his job to do and that

was all that concerned him. Castro was a dictator and he would die. The revolution would go on and he, Fenton, would join it.

In time, Manuel, or someone like him, would be the dictator—probably as despotic a one as Castro, perhaps worse. But that was no concern of Fenton's.

He would be dead before it happened.

eight

It was a short while past midnight on the first of January, 1959. Fulgencio Batista loaded a limousine with his luggage. His second wife and three of his children were with him, ready to leave the presidential estate at Kuquine. Batista said farewell to his servants, told them that the family was off on a brief trip. Then, with his limousine flanked by secret service cars carrying troops with submachine guns, the dictator headed for Camp Columbia.

Within two hours, Batista's plane was in the air, headed for sanctuary in the Dominican Republic. Like a thief in the night, the strong man of Cuba had stolen out of his own country. His time for power was over and he could now do nothing more than save his own life.

The revolution was an unqualified success. The following day Castro and his bearded followers rode in triumph through the streets of every principal city of the islands. Crowds thronged after them, screaming Castro's name at the tops of their lungs. The Twenty-sixth of July Movement, a movement pledged to the hilt to freedom and liberty, had triumphed.

The victory of Castro was the defeat of Castro. The shouts of acclaim for the revolution were that revolution's death-knell. Because men who win wars are poor at making peace, and men who win fame as rebels are all too often unequal to the task of governing the land they have liberated. The switch from traitor to hero is too sudden, the new role too difficult to play properly.

There have been exceptions—George Washington in America, for one. But the exceptions are few and far between. It is all too simple for the men who overthrow dictators to step nimbly into the dictator's shoes, all too easy for the liberator to place his own chains upon his nation.

In December of 1958 Fidel Castro was an outlaw, had been an outlaw for five and one-half years. In January of 1959 he was a national hero, an acknowledged leader. A greater man might have shaved his rebel beard, might have stepped down from the pedestal on which his country had placed him, might have denounced the Communists in his mushrooming band —as he had once accepted help from the Communists at the university and then turned against them—and then called at once for honest elections and for an end to terror. But most men would have done exactly what Fidel Castro did. Power was waiting, and he accepted it.

He was a hero now, known the world over. American magazines placed his picture on their covers. Cubans cheered his every word. Khrushchev fed his ego. The South American countries feared him. The United States, unfortunately, handled him with kid gloves, immobilized by concern over world opinion.

But Fidel charged forward, sure he was invincible, the man of the hour. Sure he had made promises, promises which seemed simple enough when he was a brigand in the hills of Oriente, broadcasting words of hope over the rebel station to hopeful listeners everywhere. But now that Batista was out and Castro was in, those same promises were much harder to keep than they had been to make.

In May of 1958 he had told Cuba: "Personally, I do not aspire to any post and I consider that there is sufficient proof that I fight for the good of my people, without any personal or egotistic ambition soiling my conduct. After the revolution we will convert the movement into a political party and we will fight with the arms of the constitution and the law. Not even then will I aspire to the presidency because I am only thirty-one years old."

Had he meant that, or was it his way of blinding Cubans to his real purpose? At first, his words seemed genuine, for he appointed Manuel Urrutia as provisional president of Cuba, with general elections planned within the year. Then he deposed Urrutia and postponed those elections indefinitely. They were never held.

It seemed simpler to take the quick way, the easy way. He had the power and the nation was willing to follow wherever he led. Why bother with elections? Why wait for laws? He excused himself, saying that he would have to retain power until the revolution was a reality and until all reforms had been achieved. He kept his beard and went on wearing the uniform of a guerrilla fighter. Liberty and freedom could wait—or be shunted aside forever.

This was the first step, the suspension of the machinery of democracy. Next came the elimination of judicial processes. The country overflowed with former associates and lieutenants of Batista. Fidel had a simple answer. He put them before the firing squads. It was, once again, revolutionary justice. The term called into being with executions in the hills was revived now. Trials were dispensed with, the excuse being that they took time. Men were arrested quickly and systematically. They were brought before a revolutionary tribunal which pronounced them guilty. Then they were taken to the courtyard where the firing squad waited.

There were precedents, of course. The Committee of Public Safety, with its reign of terror that sent thousands to the guillotine in eighteenth-century France. The Russian Revolution, with mass executions of czarist officers. Castro called the process revolutionary justice, but it turned out to be another name for terror.

*He was no better than the man he had deposed—
Batista.*

The executions drew protest and alienated supporters, particularly in the United States. Fidel Castro
could not understand the criticism. "Batista never gave
anyone a trial," he said. "He just had them killed, and
there were no protests or criticisms then. These men
are murderers, assassins. We are not executing inno-
cent people or political opponents. We are executing
murderers and they deserve to be shot."

Perhaps they did, but Batista executed for the same
reason—to kill opposition. And methods which are
legitimate for a guerilla band are not legitimate for a
government.

Just as Castro's domestic policies gave democracy a
back seat, so did his foreign policy draw him further
and further from the United States. He had stated fre-
quently that he would confiscate no foreign property,
that he was not a Communist, that the United States
was no enemy of his. But his position began to change.
American business interests kept leveling a charge of
Communism at Castro. The American press echoed
this charge. Castro denied vehemently these accusa-
tions.

But he seized oil refineries and took over land owned
by Americans. He accused the United States of crime
after crime, using America as a convenient scapegoat
to justify every extreme measure of his own. Every day

saw him drawing further from the West and moving closer and closer to the Communist bloc. He saw an enemy in everyone who disagreed with him, a potential danger in every casual opponent.

He had thrown out a dictator. Now he had become a dictator himself. The Cuban people still backed him, still worshipped him. But the seeds of discontent had been sown.

nine

Señora Luchar was talking. They were in the living room, she and Turner and Hines, and they were drinking the inevitable demitasse cups of strong black coffee. Hines couldn't stand the coffee, or Señora Luchar, or Turner, or anyone else in the world, himself least of all. His fingers gripped the small white cup so tightly he was afraid it would break in his hand. He wished he was a smoker; a cigarette would be good right now, but it seemed a silly time to start.

"Today is the twentieth of July," Señora Luchar was saying. "Tomorrow Castro makes his trip across the island. Thursday he speaks in Santiago, a speech to workers and peasants. Then he returns here, to Havana, in time for his speech commemorating the anniversary of the Twenty-sixth of July Movement. He'll be speaking Sunday, in the main square. That's not far from here. You know where it is?"

Hines nodded.

"So that's the time," the Luchar woman said. "There will be a huge crowd, too huge for the police to do much good. You're using bombs, right? Bombs that you throw?"

"That's right," Hines told her.

"So you mingle with the crowd and throw the bombs. Then you get away and return here. We'll get you back to the mainland."

"It sounds shaky," Turner broke in.

"Mr. Turner?"

"Yeah," Turner went on. "Yeah, it sounds shaky. We're right in the middle of it. It's not tough tossing the bombs. It's tough getting away."

The woman looked at him.

"We're taking a chance," Turner said.

"Of course. And you are being paid how much to take this chance? Twenty thousand dollars? You would not be paid so much if there were no chance, Mr. Turner."

She turned, left them. Turner shrugged and headed for the stairs to the basement. Hines got up, not particularly anxious to follow Turner. But where the hell else was he supposed to go?

Turner said: "What do you think of the setup?"

"I don't know."

"We'll be sitting ducks. If we play it the way she calls it, we'll be deader than hell before the bomb goes off. I don't like it."

"So?"

Turner hesitated, then stated boldly, "I want out, Jim."

"You must be kidding."

"No, I mean it."

"You?" Hines was on his feet now, his eyes amazed.

This was too much, he thought. Big old Turner, tough guy Turner, the desperate desperado. *He* wanted out.

"Me."

"Why? Getting cold feet, for God's sake? Going chicken?"

"Uh-huh."

"Well, I don't get it."

Turner shrugged. "There's not a hell of a lot to get. I took this job to beat a stateside murder rap. I was going to run for Brazil. Well, why Brazil? I'm in Cuba. I can stay here."

"Stay here?"

"Get work, find a place to live. I don't know. I like it here, Jim. And I'm here already. Why commit another murder so I can start running all over again?"

"Jesus Christ. What would you *do* here, for God's sake?"

"Anything. There's a lot of new construction going up—and I've swung construction work before. I know how to handle heavy equipment and they're short of that kind of labor."

"So you'll throw away twenty grand to work a steam shovel? That doesn't sound like you, Turner."

"Maybe not. Or maybe it does, I don't know. And there's a guy I got friendly with, a grifter type. He wants me to throw in with him. He works some semi-legitimate cons and he makes a living. And it sounds a hell of a lot better to me than tossing bombs around like an imitation anarchist. Castro's not my enemy. He may be bad, but it doesn't make a hell of a lot of difference to me. All I want is a nice quiet place to live, food to eat, liquor to drink and a woman when I need one. I can get all those no matter who's in charge here."

"So you're quitting."

"Maybe."

Hines went over to his bunk, sat down. He was sweating. First the truth about Joe and now Turner doing a fadeout, gumming up the works by quitting cold on him. It was all falling apart at the seams—his whole little world.

He didn't know how to tie it together again.

"Jesus," he said. "What am I supposed to do now?"

"That's up to you."

"I can't go ahead and throw the bomb—"

"Sure you can. I'll put it together for you. It only takes one person to heave it. If we both go, it only makes it easier for them to spot us."

"But—"

"You can even take my share of the dough. That makes it forty thou instead of twenty."

"*I don't care about the money!*"

"Hey," Turner said. "Calm down, kid."

"You don't know, damn you. You don't understand a goddamn thing."

"What are you talking about?"

"About everything. Joe was my brother, damn it, and Castro killed him. So I have to kill Castro. Can't you get that into your fat head?"

"So kill him! I don't care—"

"*Goddamn* it! You know what I found out, Turner? Castro had a right to kill Joe. Joe was a turncoat, he got power happy and tried a coup of his own. Do you hear what I'm saying? I'm over here getting some kind of cockeyed revenge for my hero of a brother who had it coming all along! Isn't that one for the goddamned books? Here I am living in a cruddy cellar and scheming like some kind of comic-strip character and it's all for revenge. And Joe doesn't deserve being avenged in the first place. How do you like that, Turner? And what the hell am I supposed to do now?"

He sat there, glaring. He was waiting for Turner to say something but the older man was silent, watching him with cool eyes. He felt like a nut now, like some kind of an idiot. He'd been shouting at the top of his lungs like a kid with a tantrum.

"Jim—"

"I'm sorry, Turner. I lost control."

"Forget it. Jim, get the hell out of here. I didn't know about Joe. How did you find out?"

"From the Luchar broad."

"Are you sure she was telling it straight?"

"Yeah. I've checked around and…oh, hell, she wouldn't have any reason to lie to me. If she was going to lie she'd do it the other way, Turner. She'd want me to stay revenge-happy so I wouldn't blow the assassination. She wasn't lying. It's straight. Joe must have gone a little nutty or something. He probably lost his edge the same way Castro did. Power does that to a person. It happens all through history. But it takes a little of the steam out of…out of *me*, damn it. It's like shooting the governor because your brother went to the chair for a murder he committed. It makes it silly."

"Yeah."

"Turner? What do I do now?"

"What I told you. Get the hell out."

"Out of Cuba?"

"Uh-huh. Get the first boat back to the States and stay there. You're not a criminal, kid. You're young, you can go back to school and start fresh. You've got a story to save up and tell your own kids someday. In the meantime you can live instead of dying. Because if you stay in Havana they're going to kill you, Jim. This game was a last chance for me. I figured there might be a nice easy way to bump Castro and stay alive. But there isn't, and I can stay alive without it."

"But—"

"And so can you. Look, you don't care about the money. Remember? And the revenge seems kind of pointless now. So throw your hand in."

"I don't know."

Turner took out a cigarette, lit it. He took a deep drag, let the smoke out in a thin stream. The air in the cellar was dense and the smoke stayed in a long, snakelike column as it rose slowly to the ceiling.

"I'll tell you what I'm going to do," he said.

"Go ahead," begged Hines.

"I'm staying right here until Saturday. There are three other guys in on this, don't forget. God knows where they are, but they're supposed to be somewhere around here in Cuba. Ray Garrison, Matt Garth, Earl Fenton. You remember them?"

"I remember."

"Yeah. Well, there's no law saying we have to be the ones to hit Castro. They might get him first. If that happens, we have our twenty grand apiece without any risk. So I'm sticking around to see if maybe that'll happen. It would be nice."

Hines didn't say anything.

"Saturday night," Turner went on, "I clear out. Don't ask where I'm going because I wouldn't be able to tell you. I'll hole up somewhere for the time being so that Lady Luchar and her hired hands can't decide they don't like me any more. Then I'll apply for Cuban citizenship. I'll go straight to the government and tell them I'm wanted for murder in the States and I like the climate better in Cuba. I'll have a work permit the same day and a set of citizenship papers within the week. And I'll be set."

"And what should I do, Turner?"

"Stick around until Saturday. You don't want to miss out on twenty grand, do you?"

"I told you—"

"That you don't care about the money. I got that. But you wouldn't throw it away if someone dropped it in your lap, would you?"

"No," Hines admitted.

"Fine. So you hang around until Saturday. Then you grab a boat or a plane, go to the Swiss consulate and tell them you're an American refugee, something like that. They'll get you back to Miami and you can go it alone from there."

"That's the sensible way, huh?"

"Sure."

Hines nodded to himself. There was always a sensible way, and there was another way that seemed more honest. He decided it was a hell of a shame that the honest way was never the sensible way.

"Will you put those bombs together? And explain to me how they work?"

"Why—"

"Saturday night," Hines went on desperately, doggedly. "Saturday night you'll show me how the bombs work. Sunday you can disappear. I don't care. Because Sunday I'm going to blow the hell out of Castro."

"Didn't you hear a thing I said? Don't you remember what *you* said, goddamn it?"

"I remember."

"Then—"

"I don't even want to talk about it. I know—I'll be getting killed, maybe, and all for a brother who had it coming. But I don't want to think about it, it only makes my head ache. I can't take it any more. I don't know what's right or wrong, Turner. I can't tell the heroes from the villains. It's not black and white like a morality play. It's all kinds of shades of gray."

Turner dropped his cigarette to the floor. He covered it with his foot and ground it out. He did not say anything.

"All shades of gray," Hines went on. "And it all boils down to the same thing. He killed my brother and I'm going to kill him. That's what I keep winding up with. I can't take the boat back to the States, I can't run like a rat to the Swiss consulate. I have to wait here and I have to blow that bastard in two with a bomb. That's all I can do."

It was Wednesday morning. Maria boiled a huge pot of water over a small fire of brush and twigs. She tossed a cup or two of coffee grounds into the pot and let it boil for ten minutes. Then she ladled out cups of the hot, black coffee. Fenton took one and walked a short distance away with it, sat down and got a cigarette going while the coffee cooled a little.

It was Wednesday morning. Castro would pass along the road late in the afternoon or early in the evening. A young boy had brought the news the night before, a twelve-year-old kid with hollow eyes and beads of perspiration on his brow, who ran through the underbrush like a startled deer. Late in the afternoon or early in the evening—that was the word from the underground, passed from mouth to mouth in whispers, brought this last step of the way by this boy with hollow eyes.

Late in the afternoon, early in the evening. Fenton sucked smoke from his cigarette, took a tentative sip of the steaming coffee. He burned his mouth and cursed quietly. Late in the afternoon, early in the evening. He was as tense as a tightly coiled spring, jumpy as a hand grenade with the pin pulled. Late in the afternoon, early in the evening.

Tomorrow Castro spoke in Santiago. Or, if they were successful, tomorrow Castro spoke to the dead, spoke to other corpses in the language cadavers speak. Castro lived or died, and this would be determined soon—late in the afternoon, early in the evening.

The whole camp was rigid with a mixture of anticipation and brittle fear. The days had been bad ones lately. Tuesday, around noon, a Jeep with two soldiers in it had rolled slowly down the road. A pair of Castristas on patrol. Manuel had ordered everyone to let Jeep and soldiers pass. They could not risk exposing their position, not until the big game was in the sights of the Sten guns. A Jeep with two soldiers was no target at all when Fidel Castro himself was due to come into firing range.

But Taco Sardo forgot the order, or else ignored it. His Sten gun belched bullets over the formation of rock and the Jeep halted, a tire gone. The soldiers came out with automatic rifles in their hands, and they had to be killed at once. They could not be allowed to escape, could not be permitted to pass the word to the garrison that rebels lay in ambush along the road to Santiago.

It had been a short, desperate fight. One of the new recruits had died, a Castrista rifle bullet tearing half his face away. Garth got one of the soldiers with a Sten gun blast but the other was back in the Jeep suddenly, ready to ride to Santiago on the rims if he had to.

Two of the rebels had stopped the Jeep. Manuel shot out another tire and Taco Sardo, who had started all the trouble in the first place, quickly raced into the road to put a pistol bullet into the driver's throat.

The Jeep would not run. Four of them together managed to push it down the road a short distance. Then, with two others to assist, they lifted the crippled vehicle and carried it from the road, hiding it in the brush. They lifted the two dead soldiers and carried them far into the hills, leaving their bodies to rot. Maria scrubbed blood from the road, Fenton picked up shards of broken glass. When they were done, no evidence of the scramble remained. The road was clear again, empty.

That had been trouble enough. That alone had swelled the tension, had drawn everyone's nerves back like a bowstring.

There was more Tuesday evening. Fenton was not sure what had happened, but while he sat among the rocks and kept a lonely vigil over the road, there was a sharp scream, curses in Spanish, a roar of pain. And later that evening he saw Garth with deep scratches across his face. And Maria wore a deep frown, and her eyes were pools of bitterness.

Now Fenton drank his coffee and smoked another cigarette. It was a moot point, he thought, whether Castro's convoy would arrive before the rebels succeeded in killing each other off. Matt Garth obviously didn't learn from experience; he was going to go on until someone put a bullet in him. Taco, blood-hungry after being wounded in the leg, would shoot at anything that came within range. Manuel sat lost in thought, still the leader but now gripped by his dream of power and glory. Maria burned with fear and anger. And Earl Fenton, the quiet man, the refugee of a teller's cage in the Metropolitan Bank of Lynbrook, the man with cancer in his lungs, drank bitter coffee and smoked strong cigarettes and waited for Fidel to come and meet his death.

Late in the afternoon.

Or early in the evening.

Matt Garth liked things simple and direct. If you made things too complicated you just loused them up. When you wanted a woman, you took her. When you were killing someone for a price, you went ahead and killed him. And when you had a burn on for some son-of-a-bitch who had been giving you a hard time, well, you belted him one.

Which was what he was going to do.

He had just finished his session as lookout. He had crouched between rocks as mute and massive as Garth himself, his Sten gun perched along a rock ledge with a fresh clip in its breech. And four soldiers came rolling along in a battered Jeep, peering into the brush in a hunt for rebels. One of them, a beardless kid, had focused a pair of binoculars upon the precise spot where Garth was sitting. And Garth's finger was poised on the trigger. One burst of the Sten gun would have sent the four rat bastards to hell. But the kid with the glasses had seen nothing, and the soldiers were gone now.

So to hell with being lookout. One of the Cubans had taken over, a guy named Jiminez, and Garth didn't have to play lookout like a goddamn kid playing cops and robbers. He had better things to do.

The first thing to do was find Fenton. Fenton had it coming, all right. There was Maria, flat on her back and ready to take it and there was Garth ready to give it to her. And that buttinsky, Fenton, had to foul things up.

Garth laughed. The bastard wouldn't know what to do with a woman if she came around and tried to serve it to him on a platter, but he had to louse things up for Garth.

Well, he'd know better next time.

Garth smiled. He was still smiling when he found Fenton by the dead campfire. Fenton didn't return the smile.

"Say," he said deceptively, "I wanted to talk to you."

"What about?"

"Private stuff," Garth told him. "And listen—I'm sorry I belted you the other day. I lost my head. I got all hot over the broad and I couldn't think about nothing else."

"Oh," Fenton said. "Well, it's all right."

"No hard feelings?"

"None."

"Shake on it?"

Fenton seemed to hesitate, then accepted the huge hand offered to him. They shook hands solemnly.

"Now," Garth went on innocently, "let's talk. I got things you oughta know about."

"Then tell me."

"It's private, Earl. C'mon—let's head over into the brush a ways. These spics are all the time listening."

Fenton shrugged, stood up. He was holding the Sten gun in one hand. Garth led him away from the camp, into the brush far from the road. Garth wanted to laugh—it was getting cute now. You could take these complicated guys like Fenton and you could twist them up six ways and backwards. The simple things were best, damn it.

"What's it all about, Garth?"

"Oh, it's interesting," Garth said, stalling. "About this Castro bird. The one we hit in the head tomorrow."

"You mean today. Any minute, as a matter of fact."

"Yeah," Garth said. "Well, whenever the hell it is. It'll be a gas telling them about it on Bleecker Street, you know? Can you see it?"

"Is that all you wanted?"

"Not exactly. Lemme have your gun a minute, Earl."

Fenton handed him the gun. "Why do you want it?"

"I don't want it," Garth said, tossing the Sten gun into a clump of bushes. "I just don't want you to have it, Earl, honey. Because I'm going to beat the crap out of you, Earl."

"I don't—"

That was all he said. Garth drove a fist to the pit of his stomach, doubling him over. Then a right uppercut straightened him out again, and a left cross to the chest put him on the ground. He lay there looking as though he had been hit by a truck.

"You fell for it," Garth said. "No hard feelings? I got plenty of feelings, you son-of-a-bitch!"

He hauled Fenton up, smashed him full in the face. Fenton's nose was bleeding now. He hit him, smashed his lips, felt teeth give way. This time he let him fall to the ground. He kicked him hard, felt ribs crack and kicked him again. The man on the ground looked lifeless, inert, but Garth knew he wasn't dead. Matt Garth was a pro, damnit. He could beat the hell out of a guy and not kill him. He knew his business.

He whirled at a sound. Maria had followed them; she stood in the clearing now, gun in hand, her eyes on

Fenton. The eyes moved to Garth and stared with hatred. But Garth ignored the gun. Beating Fenton had excited him; he always got excited after a muscle job, always needed a woman as soon as possible. And here was a woman—to hell with the gun in her hand.

He rushed her. There was a moment when she could have shot him, but she hadn't expected his move and the chance was lost. His whole body slammed into her, knocking the gun from her grasp, tumbling her to the ground. He fell on her, and although she fought him she didn't have a chance. He had her where he wanted her.

Fenton wasn't going to stop him now, not this time. Nobody was going to stumble on them. This time, goddamn it, he was going to lay her silly.

He ripped off her clothes, stripping her naked, and struck her savagely in the face or stomach or naked breasts every time she tried to resist him. Then he fumbled momentarily with his own clothing, struck her again, forced her legs apart, went for her. She had given up, knowing resistance was useless, resigned to the inevitable.

He plunged deep into the soft warmth of her. She struggled anew, briefly.

And then, finally, it was over.

He got slowly to his feet. "You're hot stuff," he told Maria. "We'll have to go another round pretty soon."

Her eyes were sheer hatred.

Garth laughed. He looked at Fenton—conscious now, on his feet again, and able to function. Fenton had his gun back. And Maria moved to pick up hers.

"C'mon," he told them. "We gotta go up against this Castro guy. Then we can have some more fun."

He turned his back to them and started through the brush again, back to the camp site. Either one of them could have shot him. But he knew they would not. In both their minds, Castro came first.

And no one shot him.

Ernesto took a small sip of sour red wine. The heavyset Cuban put his glass on the table and smiled broadly.

"My friend," he said. "You have decided to stay in Cuba, true?"

"I've decided to stay," Turner said.

"And you will obtain papers? You will become a citizen?"

Turner nodded.

"A thought has come to me," Ernesto said. "I have a friend, an official in the Department of Immigration. He is not busy these days. More people seek to leave Cuba than to enter here. This friend of mine, he is a fine man. You would like him, *amigo.*"

"You have many friends, Ernesto."

"So? Can a man live without friends? Friends are the strength of a man. But to continue. This friend of mine, this official, might make matters simpler. There are complications to becoming a citizen, even in Cuba. What you Americans call pink tape."

"Red tape."

"So. My friend could cut this red tape. A preparation of papers, a signature, the application of an official seal, and you are a citizen of Cuba. Is it not simple?"

"Shall we go to this friend?"

"Very simple."

Turner considered. "I have no money," he said. "Wouldn't it cost some money for this friend to expedite things?"

Ernesto sighed, extended his hands with his palms down. "This is a friend," he said. "Not an acquaintance but a friend, as you are my friend. Once I was able to do a great service for this friend. Once he was in great trouble with the man Torelli of whom I spoke. He was a croupier, and there was the matter of a shortage. I was able to cover for my friend. Thus he would be happy to do a service for me in return. There will be no need for money in this case."

"Well," Turner said. "That's different."

"So. Let us go, my friend. And in an hour you shall be a free citizen of Cuba. Then we shall go again to the bordello, yes? I am in need of a woman. And we shall celebrate your citizenship."

Two hours later Turner was a citizen of Cuba. The three of them—he, Ernesto and the Immigration official—had a drink in celebration. Then they taxied to a bordello which Ernesto liked. Turner was happy now. He was safe. He did not have to think of murdering Castro.

Castro's convoy was sighted at seventeen minutes past six.

One of the new men had the watch. He saw the lead Jeep pull into view, saw it far off down the road. He gave the signal, and the rebel band began drifting into position, stationing themselves in strategic spots along the rock formations on either side of the road. Fenton was ready, gun in hand, heart hammering. He braced himself with his back against a boulder, then shifted and stretched prone in the gap between two huge rocks. He lay down on his belly and pointed his weapon at the road.

Time.

A Jeep with four uniformed soldiers led the procession. Directly behind it was a truck covered with a canvas top. There were men in it, Fenton knew. Soldiers, armed with rifles and machine guns and grenades. And behind the truck was another Jeep, with more soldiers.

So Castro was expecting an ambush. That was obvious—you didn't travel with the entire militia around you if you thought you were one hundred percent safe. There was a third Jeep, with more soldiers. Then a long Lincoln, a limousine, with the shades drawn.

Castro had to be in the Lincoln. He would be traveling there, behind drawn shades, probably cool and comfortable in an air-conditioned car. And there was a pair of Buicks behind the Lincoln, then a slew of Jeeps with still more soldiers.

Fenton drew a deep breath.

The convoy crawled forward. Fenton began to ache inside for a cigarette, for a cup of coffee, for something. He steadied himself, steadied his gun. It seemed now that everything had to go wrong, that the convoy could not help getting wind of the rebel trap. Fenton looked across the road, saw Manuel aiming his gun through a blind of branches arranged for camouflage. He saw Maria in the shadow of another rock, then looked to his right and listened to the heavy breathing of another rebel. God, they were too easy to see, too easy to spot! They did not stand a chance.

The lead Jeep was approaching. It was already level with Taco Sardo, who had the post furthest to the rear. Fenton listened to the motors of the Jeeps and the truck, heard a bird singing in a nearby shrub, drew in his breath sharply when he heard another rebel shift position and snap a twig. It seemed to Fenton that any sound, however slight, would be heard by Castro's forces, that any noise at all would give away the rebel position. He knew this was ridiculous but he couldn't help feeling it. He tried to hold his own breath, tried to keep from making any sound at all.

The convoy kept coming. The plan was a simple one—they were to hold fire until the lead Jeep came abreast of the position held by Garth on one side and a man named Jiminez on the other. Then they would open fire. Garth and Jiminez were to shoot down the lead vehicles, blocking the road at the front. Sardo and a few others would be doing the same to the Jeeps at the rear of the procession. That would keep Castro in the middle, would prevent the big Lincoln limousine from escaping either to the front or to the rear.

The rest was up to the rebels in the center, to Manuel and Maria and Fenton and to one or two more. They would level their guns at the Lincoln, going for Castro, for the big fish in the pond. It would be easier with a few grenades or a bazooka, Fenton thought. Something that would stop a Jeep with a single shot. It was harder when you had to make Sten guns do all the work.

And then he stopped thinking, because the time was coming.

The Lincoln was in range now. Fenton looked directly at it, looked at the gleaming metal, the drawn curtains. He steadied himself and his gun, pointing the barrel at one of the windows in the rear. At any moment Garth and Jiminez would start shooting. That would be his cue.

Damn it all, go on!

His heart stopped beating for those two seconds. He had an awful premonition of disaster and death that refused to leave his mind. His hands gripped the Sten gun shakily.

Then a shot rang out.

Fenton turned into a machine. He sprawled on his belly and held the Sten gun's trigger down, spraying bullets against the window of the Lincoln. But things happened quickly, too quickly. The government forces reacted with the speed of light, almost as if they had been waiting for the shot with the same rapt attention Fenton himself had displayed. The lead Jeep spun off the road against the rocks and soldiers piled out of it, guns in hand. The second Jeep peeled off after it, and the canvas-topped truck barreled off to the other side with men spilling out of it on the way. The bullets didn't stop Castro's limousine and the other vehicles weren't piled up in front of it. The road was unblocked.

And the Lincoln limousine went like the wind. The driver pressed the gas pedal to the floor and the big car responded magnificently with the coiled grace of a striking cobra. The car surged forward, the road clear ahead of it, and Fenton's bullets didn't seem to be having any effect at all. He tried for the tires and missed. And he knew instinctively that Castro was on the floor, that he had hit the floorboards when the first shot rang out, that he had escaped the trap.

The Lincoln didn't stop. More gunfire chased it and more gunfire failed to stop the big car. But now their fire was being returned. The soldiers in the road were caught in the middle, with rebels in the rocks on either side. But there were too many of them—fifty or more, Fenton saw, as Jeep after Jeep emptied out men with guns.

His gun chattered again and men fell in the road. He broke open the gun, put in a fresh clip, fired. Returning fire splayed the rock to one side of him as he shrank back instinctively, still holding down the Sten gun's trigger, still raining bullets on the men in the road.

Manuel's voice was high, shrill, calling for a retreat. Fenton saw Taco Sardo a short distance down the road. The boy got up to run, but this time no rifle bullet hit him in the leg. This time a machine gun chased him and a line of bullets trailed down his back from his neck to the base of his spine. Taco fell dead and the battle raged on.

Fenton scrambled to his feet, backed away into the woods. It was their only chance, he knew. The government troops would crush them in open battle, even with the superior position the rebels held. Sheer weight of numbers was too much to overcome with a positional advantage. They had to retreat, had to get back into the cover of the jungle. They knew the jungle and the Castristas did not. It was the only chance they had.

Bullets dug up the dirt at Fenton's feet. He was running now. The weeks in the jungle had toughened him, had made him wise in the ways of war and outdoor living. His feet were sure of themselves, quick and easy on the treacherous paths. He ran back in the direction of the camp, away from the road and the battle.

He saw Garth on one side of him, Maria on the other. They, too, were running. Garth charged on ahead, and Fenton saw Maria raise a pistol to shoulder height. He gaped.

The girl, running, fired the pistol. And Garth caught the bullet in the back of his head.

He pitched forward and died.

Fenton ran, found cover, took it. He steadied himself in a clump of thick brush, replaced the Sten gun's empty clip with still another one, caught his breath. So Garth was dead—Garth lived through the fighting and died because a woman on his own side hated him enough to shoot him in the back. Garth was dead, and other rebels were dead, and the government troops were still unsatisfied. They wouldn't let go, wouldn't just drive on, even though the rebel assault had been crippled. Now they were moving on, into the brush. They wanted to kill the rebels to the last man.

It looked as though they were going to.

Fenton saw Jiminez break for cover from the road. He saw a soldier pull the pin from a grenade, saw him hold it, counting quickly in Spanish. Then he watched the lazy flight of the grenade, soft and fat like a plump bird. Jiminez ran and the grenade followed. Then the grenade dropped to the ground at the feet of Jiminez and the man screamed in terror.

The explosion drowned the scream and Jiminez died in pieces.

The government soldiers pushed on. Fenton let his finger freeze on the Sten gun trigger, let it keep spitting lead at the soldiers. Men died from his bullets faster than he could count them. But there were too many of them, more than he could kill.

He saw a scene on his left, saw two of the soldiers with Manuel. Manuel, who was going to kill Castro and rule in his place. Manuel, who would be the fearless leader of the people, the force around which the enemies of Castro could rally.

Manuel, whose ambitions were drowned now.

They had Manuel. His weapon was on the ground, useless. And Manuel, hero, leader of the people, looked at death and saw its face. Manuel screamed like an injured child and tears streaked his brown face. He screamed and the soldiers laughed at him.

There were two of them. One held a gun to Manuel's temple while the other castrated Manuel with a bolo knife. Manuel passed out, fell to the ground. Then the soldier with the pistol shot him through the forehead.

Fenton cut them both down with his Sten gun.

The battle went on, halfway to forever. It was twilight, and then it was dark, and at some indeterminable time the Jeep engines roared and the Castristas left their dead behind. Fenton was still in his clump of shrubbery, still safe, still alive. No bullets had touched him. He could not believe this at first but it seemed to be true. The battle was over and he, miraculously, was alive.

He remained in position for several minutes, until the last enemy vehicle was out of sight. Then he moved from the clump of brush and looked at the carnage. Over thirty government soldiers lay dead, some in the road, others in the fields. Garth was dead, Manuel dead and mutilated, Jiminez dead, Taco dead—

Maria was alive. He found her, moaning, in a thicket not far from him. She had been wounded twice. There was a bullet in her abdomen; another bullet had shattered her left leg. She moaned and cursed in Spanish.

He put a splint on her leg. He dug out the bullets from her body, bandaged her wounds. He lit the campfire again and made some soup for her but she refused to eat. He tended her, trying to make her comfortable.

She died around midnight. He sat alone by the fire, smoking a cigarette he had taken from one of the corpses. He was alone, the last remnant. He—the doomed man, the man who had to die. He was alive.

It seemed unfair.

It was late when he fell asleep. In the morning he awoke when the sun struck his eyes. He got to his feet, made himself a quick breakfast, and left the area.

The last survivor. Now he had to go on, to kill and kill and kill. The cancer was a strong pain over his heart—it would not let him live long, and soon he could stop killing and fighting and running. Soon the cancer would kill him, or the Castristas would kill him. From one side or another, death would come.

When it did, it would be a release.

ten

No man in history ever had an easier time taking power than did Fidel Castro when Batista fled the country leaving him the keys to the kingdom. Castro had, from the beginning, the one ingredient Batista never attained in all his years of despotism. He had the people behind him.

There were dissident elements. The political henchmen who had grown fat under Batista did not welcome the bearded rebel, certainly. And the very rich—the large landowners, the growers of tobacco and sugar—knew that Castro's regime would mean a financial loss to them. But the people of Cuba, the lawyers and the doctors and the shopkeepers and the students and the workers and the peasants, backed the revolution all the way. Castro was their leader and they were his people.

It is not easy to become hated by people who love you. It is not a simple matter to switch positions entirely, so that those who supported you once now seek to destroy you. Castro did not do this all at once. He did not even manage it entirely.

American support went first. The United States was quick to distrust Castro—and with good reason. His several reforms too soon became just another form of oppression. True, some peasants did get land, some efforts were made in the direction of combating the problem of poverty. But with those reforms came oppressions and seizures of people and property that equaled Batista's earlier brutalities.

Fidel could have changed American popular opinion, but the years in the hills had not made a subtle compromiser out of him. Charging forward like an enraged, clumsy bull might work in guerrilla warfare, but he tried to apply that method to international diplomacy.

The United States was used as the excuse and cause for every failing in Cuba, the germ responsible for every last one of the island's ills. Castro shouted that Batista's men had held power at the wheels of American tanks, firing American guns and dropping bombs from American planes. He brought truths, half-truths and lies together in such a way that Cuban popular opinion quickly turned anti-American. But the price of this was the friendship of the United States, which he lost.

The United States cut the Cuban sugar quota, a fairly drastic move which could have wrecked the Cuban economy. Castro traded with Russia. The confiscated American refineries were used to process Soviet oil, and the Russians bought the Cuban sugar— at a drastically reduced price. Castro ordered the staff of the American Embassy in Havana cut to one-tenth, overnight, and the inevitable result was a break in diplomatic relations between the two nations.

In Fidel Castro's mind, all of this was desirable, all of it justified. He was moving toward paranoia, the most common personality disorder of the dictator, in which treacherous enemies are seen around every corner. Castro had defined his enemies within his own mind. The United States was persecuting him and he would stand fast against this enemy.

He moved on, further and further from reality, leaving former supporters behind along the way. The middle classes grew disillusioned first. Hard and fast supporters of Castro in the beginning, the educated professionals were quick to realize that the man they had backed in the fight against Batista was simply a tyrant of a different sort. These Cubans wanted freedom, but they did not want radical economic changes leading to a socialistic economy, nor did they want to see Cuba take her place at Russia's side.

Cuba's middle class was small. The economic order that Batista had fostered had little place for the bourgeoisie—there were rich men and there were poor men, with few in the middle. But the Cuban middle class had raised money for Castro, had helped him when he most needed help. Now they were running out on him.

They went to Miami, to Tampa. They went by boat or by plane, with legal visas or as secret refugees. And Castro rationalized their desertion by moving further to the left. The bourgeoisie had no place in a true socialistic order, he argued. Cuba was better without them.

Other revolutionaries followed in their footsteps. Men who had fought at Castro's side, men who had been willing to give their lives in the fight against Batista, now saw they had made no great bargain. Some of them were hopeless idealists, men who would be content with nothing less than perfection, men who would rebel against any established order. But still more of them were honest men who could not live with their conscience while Castro was at the helm.

Some of these, too, went to Miami and Tampa and New York. Some gave up on Cuba, divorcing themselves entirely from Cuban politics and applying for citizenship in the United States. But others refused to give up. They raised funds for a second revolution, trained secret armies in Florida and in Guatemala just as Castro had trained his band of eighty-two rebels in the fields of Mexico.

Members of Castro's government deserted him. Newspapers printed articles and editorials of which he disapproved, and he retaliated by suppressing those newspapers and silencing their editors. Batista had done this, branding the editors as Communist party hacks. Castro did the same thing, calling the editors the lackeys of American imperialism. The catch-words were changed but the facts remained the same. Freedom of the press and freedom of speech were on the way out. Despotism was there to stay.

And the resistance began.

It was an intelligent resistance, a keen-edged resistance. The men who were sick of Castro had learned from Castro. They knew how guerrilla warfare worked. They understood the junction of a metropolitan underground. They knew just what to do and how to do it in order to bring about the end of a man named Fidel Castro.

Once again, men with guns stole into the hills of Oriente Province, shooting Castro's soldiers from ambush, burning cane fields and spreading discontent. Once again men touched off bombs at night in Havana. The people had not yet risen against Castro. A great many Cubans still supported him. His aura was still visible to some eyes, and his halo, though fading rapidly, was still discernible to the diehards.

But the process had begun.

There was an invasion. It was supported by the Central Intelligence Agency of the United States, and it was also supported by former Batistianos—but Castro crushed this invasion. The precise details may never be known, but the invasion was a masterpiece of poor planning on the part of the invaders and the American government. The propaganda value for Castro was immense. For months he had been shouting about an American-sponsored invasion, and now it had happened.

But the tall bearded man had not learned. He

offered to trade prisoners for tractors, a move that showed a total disregard for human life. He lost the propaganda he had gained and more. Latin American supporters deserted him. Bit by bit he was cutting off friends and adding enemies.

The end was close.

eleven

Garrison went to the airline office on Saturday afternoon. He was wearing the cord suit, a lightweight white shirt, a narrow tie with a quiet foulard pattern. He stopped to light a cigarette, taking a quick look at the three open ticket counters, studying the clerks on duty. One was a girl, young and attractive. A second was a man about twenty-three, bright-eyed and alert, looking proud of his uniform. Garrison went to the third, a fortyish Cuban with a soiled shirt front. The man looked easiest to bribe.

"I want two tickets on a Miami plane tomorrow night," he said. "Got a pair open?"

The clerk checked his book, admitted that a pair of seats to Miami did in fact exist for a flight leaving Havana Airport at 7:15.

"That's fine," Garrison said. He pushed his forged identification paper to the clerk. The man scanned the white slip and nodded approval.

"For two tickets," the clerk said, "you must have two papers."

"I only have mine," Garrison said. "My friend is not with me at the moment."

The clerk sighed. "It is a rule," he said.

"A rule which could not be eased?"

The clerk thought it over. Garrison reached for his wallet, managed to open it and extract several bills without making a show of it. He could have bought another forged paper from the old forger on La Avenida Blanco, but he had guessed that it would be simpler and cheaper to bribe the airlines clerk. He put two American twenties on the counter, thought for a moment, then added another twenty to the pile.

The bills vanished. The clerk produced the pair of tickets and sold them to Garrison. Garrison paid with Cuban bills, pocketed his change.

"You must be at the airport by seven," the clerk said.

"Fine," Garrison said. "There won't be any problem at the airport?"

"Not if you have tickets."

Garrison nodded. He turned and left the airline office, caught a taxi to the Nacional. He stopped at the bar for a drink and nursed it for half an hour. It was a daiquiri, crisp and cool. He sipped his drink and patted the pocket that held his airplane tickets. There might be additional trouble at the airport, of course, but another twenty dollars or so would cure the trouble.

It was all a matter of timing, he thought. Planning and timing, that was the whole thing. The guy who said you couldn't have your cake and eat it was a man who didn't work things out carefully enough. If you timed things right, there was no reason in the world why you couldn't do both.

He ordered another drink, sat over it for ten minutes more, then wandered into the Nacional casino. He won thirty dollars at roulette, lost ten at the crap table, put five more into the slots. He left the casino fifteen dollars to the good, went to the hotel restaurant and spent most of his winnings on a steak dinner. The steak wasn't quite as rare are he liked it but it was good meat and his appetite was excellent.

He smoked a cigar with his coffee. The waiter brought him an English newspaper and he read the latest story on the attempt on Castro's life, the ambush that misfired in Oriente. Castro's limousine had sped to safety in Santiago, leaving the rebels and a detachment of government regulars to battle it out along the roadside. Garrison scanned the story quickly. Nothing much was new—the Communists were claiming the assassination attempt was an American plot, calling attention to the American who had been killed with the rebel forces. There was no identification of the corpse, but the description seemed to fit Matt Garth.

Garrison finished his coffee, folded the newspaper. So they'd tried once, he thought. And they had failed. Well, it figured. He'd been half-hoping one of the other clowns would make things easy for him by shooting Castro and saving him the trouble. Wishful thinking. He had to do it himself, and it had been a waste of money to hire the other four men in the first place. He would kill Castro, and he would wind up with the money and with Estrella, and that would be that.

He paid his check and left a tip. He went outside, walked along the street and around the block, finishing his cigar and tossing the butt into the gutter. On the way back to the hotel he passed the plaza, saw the steps of the Palace of Justice where Castro would speak. They had erected stands where some spectators would be able to sit, had barricades to prevent a mob from starting a riot that might endanger Castro's life.

Garrison laughed softly. They hadn't done anything about the windows in the Hotel Nacional. And his window was in the perfect spot. All the barricades in the world wouldn't stop his rifle bullet.

"Garth is dead," Turner said.

Hines looked at him. "How do you know?"

"I heard the radio. It's all over the country, for Christ's sake. You'd be better off if you could speak the language."

"Well, what—?"

"Rebel ambush in the east," Turner said curtly. "It flopped. Castro got through and the ambush force was wiped out. The next day they found a dead American in the middle of things."

"It was Garth?"

"They didn't give his name," Turner said. "But the description fits him. The older fellow—Fenton—was with him, the way I remember it. Fenton must have gotten away."

Hines didn't say anything. Turner let his cigarette fall from his lips to the basement floor. He stepped on it, his hands busy with the casing of the bomb. This was his role. He was preparing the bomb, getting it ready for Hines. Then he would leave, would fade into the city and make a home for himself there. He was out the twenty grand now. If the ambush had worked he would have collected it, but now it didn't matter; even if Hines was successful, he himself was out of the picture. He was a Cuban citizen and that was that.

He sighed, put the bomb down. "Garth is dead," he repeated. "Do you want to die, Jim?"

"Damnit—"

"Because you will," he went on. "Win, lose, or draw, you'll never get out of Cuba alive. You probably won't get Castro in the first place. The bomb won't go off."

"You sure of that?"

"No. I did my best with it and it should explode on impact. But I don't know a hell of a lot about bombs. It might turn out to be a dud."

"And it might set off an earthquake in Chile. Don't tell me everything that *might* happen, Turner. It doesn't scare me."

Turner shook out another cigarette and lit it. "All right," he said. "Suppose you luck out and the bomb goes off. Suppose you heave it in the right place and you get Castro. Then what?"

"I give up. What?"

"Then they tear you to pieces, you damned fool. You won't get out of the crowd. They'll eat you alive."

"You're nuts."

"And if you get away, you still won't make it out of the country. You think the Luchar babe will lift a finger for you? She doesn't give a damn if you live or die. She's a fanatic and fanatics only care about their cause. She wants you to kill Castro. She doesn't give a flying damn what happens to you after that."

Hines didn't say anything.

"Do you want to die, Jim?"

"Go to hell, Turner."

"Jim—"

Hines was next to him now. Hines reached out a hand, took the cigarette from Turner's lips, dropped it and squashed it. "I ought to belt you," Hines said. "I ought to slug you in the mouth."

"Go ahead."

"You chickened out," Hines went on. "Fine. That's your business and not mine. But I made a hell of a mistake about you, Turner. I really did. Remember that first night. I had you pegged as a guy with guts. I thought, hell, here's a guy who's been around, who knows things. I thought you were a real man."

"I changed a lot."

"No kidding. You—"

"I learned how to relax. I stopped being hunted. It makes a difference, Jim."

"You chickened out."

Turner didn't say anything. He hadn't expected to convince Hines but it didn't hurt to try. And he hadn't expected to change Hines' mind about going through with the bombing, but again it hadn't hurt him to try. If Hines tossed the bomb he was going to get killed. And Turner didn't want to see that happen. He liked the kid.

Hines said: "I'm not chickening out. You can't scare me, damnit. You give me a load of crap about the chance of getting away. You think I don't know that? You think I haven't been over it a hundred times in my mind? I figure I have one chance in ten of getting away from the plaza. God knows what kind of chance I have of getting out of Cuba; I haven't even bothered thinking about that part of it yet. I can't let myself think any further than killing Castro. I can't afford to. Whatever happens afterward will happen, and that's all. But don't try to scare me. It won't work."

Turner didn't say anything for a minute or two. He lit another cigarette, smoked in silence.

Then he said: "I didn't mean to get on your back, Jim."

"I know."

"I was trying to make it easier. Not harder."

"I know that." Hines turned away. "You want to make me save myself. I understand. And I'm sorry I called you chicken. That's a pretty silly word, isn't it? I don't know anything about courage, Turner. About bravery, heroism, all that jazz. Sometimes I get the feeling that there's no such thing as a brave man. A guy does what he has to do and no more. You've got an out now. You can stay in Cuba and enjoy yourself. Without that out you'd be braver than hell. If you've got a guy cornered then he's brave. I guess that's the way it works."

"Maybe, Jim."

Hines studied the floor, shifted his weight from one foot to the other. "You want to know something? I'm not even sure any more if I'm getting back at...at Castro because of Joe. Joe was always my big hero, you know, and I had this image of the little brother evening things up for the big brother. That part of it doesn't fit any more."

Turner said nothing.

"So I don't know why I want to kill Castro. Maybe because he ruined my hero for me, maybe some cock-eyed reason like that. I don't know. It's just something I have to do."

"Sure."

"Turner? That bomb'll go off, won't it?"

"It ought to."

"You said something about it turning out to be a dud. Was that just crap?"

"Probably. It should work. But don't stand around waiting for it, Jim. Throw it and get the hell out."

"I will."

Turner stood awkwardly for a moment. Then he clapped a hand on Hines' shoulder. "Luck," he said. "I hope you make it."

"Thanks."

He turned quickly, took the stairs two at a time. Señora Luchar was alone in the living room. She asked him if he wanted coffee.

"No thanks," he said. "I thought I'd go for a walk."

"Just a walk?"

"A long walk," he said. "I'll be staying at a hotel to-night. I'll meet Hines at the plaza tomorrow. It's safer that way."

Her eyes regarded him coolly. "Sit down," she said. "Have a cup of coffee before you go."

He had coffee with her. She talked about trivial matters until he had finished the coffee. He watched her, listened to her. Jim was right, he decided. She was like Madame Defarge in the book. She should be knitting a shawl.

"Castro will die tomorrow," she said.

"I hope so."

"He had better," she said.

Her tone accused him of everything from original sin to the crucifixion of Christ. He pretended not to notice the implication in her words, stood up, thanked her for the coffee, left. The old man was still rocking on the porch. Turner smiled at him and kept walking.

He checked into a residential hotel. His citizenship papers were in his wallet and he looked at them in the privacy of his hotel room, smiling quietly to himself. Then he went out to meet Ernesto. He walked easily, arms swinging freely at his sides. He was a free man now. He was safe. Tomorrow Hines would live or die, and tomorrow Fidel Castro would live or die, but neither of these lives or deaths were any of his concern any longer. He had done what he could do.

Now he had his own life to live.

Garrison was alone until a few minutes after ten. This evening, however, was different from all the other evenings he had spent alone. Other nights he had relaxed, listening to music, taking things easy. Tonight he was tense. He paced the floor, walked back and forth until he thought he was going to wear out the carpet or walk the heels off his shoes. He went again and again to the window to look out across to the steps of the Palace of Justice.

It was the night before the job.

But that was no reason to be tense. He had always been the icy one, the man who could eat a heavy meal, go out and commit murder for a fee, then go home and have another big meal and sleep soundly for ten straight hours. The perfect emotionless, steel-nerved killer. The pro, with a good professional attitude and solid, perpetual calmness.

And now he was tense. Tense, nervous, edgy. Somebody down the hall slammed a window shut and he nearly jumped off the edge of the bed. Tense, nervous, edgy. Three or four times he opened the dresser drawer and took out the bottle of light rum, but each time he put it away. Solitary drinking was bad any time, especially bad the night before a job. And he didn't need a drink that badly.

When Estrella came at thirteen minutes after ten he drew her inside, closed and bolted the door, found two clean water tumblers in the bathroom and filled them each a third of the way with light rum. They touched glasses and drank the liquor. Her eyes questioned him but he only smiled back at her.

They drank the rum, drained their glasses, put them down. Garrison reached for the girl and she came into his arms quickly and eagerly, her mouth raised for his kiss, her hard breasts thrusting into his chest. He held her close, kissed her. Her tongue darted out, plunged into his mouth. Her arms were tight around him, holding him.

He undressed her, undressed himself. She stretched out on the bed and he lay beside her, fondling her breasts, kissing her, telling her now that he loved her. He was surprised by the way the words felt to him. They felt true; more, he had to say them.

Preliminaries were over quickly. The need was too great now; he couldn't wait to have her, couldn't kiss and stroke, couldn't help throwing himself upon her and stabbing into her, needing the warmth of her embrace, needing the way her passion rose to meet his own.

It was fundamentally different this time. Far more

intense, although that seemed impossible to Garrison. And this time, far more necessary, far more essential. He *needed* the girl in his arms, needed her with him, near him.

It was the need that assured him that he was playing things correctly. Need was something new. All along, from the early years in Birch Fork through the war years to the present, Ray Garrison had never needed anyone. He was always his own man, always a lone man in an alien world. Now...

He could not leave her in Cuba.

Afterward, while she lay stretched out on the bed in the warm afterglow of love, he walked to his dresser, took the wallet from one of the top drawers.

"What you doing, 'arper?"

He took out the two airplane tickets and passed them to her.

"To Miami?" she asked, her voice uncertain, tremulous.

"That's right," he said. "To Miami. We're leaving tomorrow night. You have to be at the airport by seven. I'll meet you there."

"Tomorrow?"

"Tomorrow," he said. "*Mañana noche.* At the airport, at seven o'clock. Can you remember that?"

"I remember," she said. Her eyes were bright, happy. "I love you, 'arper."

"Yeah," he said. "You've got to go now, honey. Put your clothes on and go back to wherever the hell you live. And don't come here tomorrow. Go straight to the airport. Be there on time. Hell, get there early so there's no chance of a foul-up. I'll meet you."

"Okay. I love you, 'arper."

"Then why the hell are you crying?"

"Because I am 'appy."

He sat next to her, kissed the tears from her eyes. He held her, patted her. Her eyes adored him.

"You better get going," he said.

"Don' you wan' me to stay tonight?"

"Not tonight," he said.

She pouted.

"We'll have plenty of nights," he told her. "We'll go to America. We'll have the rest of our lives, Estrella. I have to be alone tonight, and tomorrow. I'll meet you at the airport."

She was a woman who knew better than to argue. She kissed him, got dressed, kissed him again, took the tickets, and left. By the time she was out the door he wanted to go after her, to tell her he had changed his mind and that he wanted her to stay. He took another quick jolt of rum instead and walked once more to the window. The shade was drawn. He raised it and squinted out through the darkness.

Less than twenty hours. He would have to shoot Castro by six. Then the gun would go back into the mattress, and then he'd hurry downstairs and take a taxi to the airport. Estrella would be there. The plane would take them to Miami, where they would pick up the money from Hiraldo. It would be twenty-five grand at least, since Garth's share would get re-distributed. Maybe more—maybe thirty-three, if Garth's partner caught a bullet of his own.

That meant no more jobs, no more of the gun-for-hire routine. With that much capital, plus the several grand he had in banks around the country, he could open some kind of business, could buy himself a soft touch that would let him retire from the trigger-pulling racket.

He tried to go to sleep but it didn't work out. He wasn't relaxed enough to sleep; the job loomed in front of him, worrying him, and his eyes stayed open. He gave up, switched the light on and got a cigarette going.

He wished the job was over and done with. It scared him, this one, and it was the first job to have such an effect upon him. He'd pulled plenty of tougher ones, had filled contracts for the syndicate that made this particular hit child's play in comparison. But this was the one that had him on edge.

He knew why.

On the other jobs, before Estrella, he had been on his own, rootless, empty. Now he had something to lose.

Saturday night Earl Fenton stormed the garrison at San Luis.

He did this alone, because he was alone now. He had been living for two days in the hills; living alone, traveling alone, sleeping alone. He had been living with cancer inside him, living with the sure foreknowledge of death and with the memory of the death of others. The memory of carnage, of Maria shooting Garth in the head, of Manuel screaming before they castrated him, of Jiminez blown to pieces by a grenade, of Maria growing weaker and weaker until she died in his arms.

He moved in silence through the hills. His Sten gun stayed always in his hands, and over his shoulder he carried a musette bag with extra clips for the gun and what food he had been able to salvage from the camp. The pain of the cancer was bad now. The disease was spreading like wildfire through his whole body, and there were times when he would cough uncontrollably while arrows of pain shot through his flesh.

Saturday, around midnight, he made his attack. San Luis was a small town a few miles to the north of Santiago. There was a detachment of soldiers stationed there. Fenton attacked them.

He killed the sentry with a knife. He crept up behind the man on silent feet, plunging the knife he had taken from a corpse into the throat of the sentry who was to become a corpse in his turn. The man died in silence and Fenton stole into one of the barracks.

He sprayed the interior with the Sten gun. He killed fourteen men before a single one of them was entirely awake. Most of them died in their sleep. The rest opened their eyes momentarily and closed them forever.

The gunfire brought soldiers from the other barracks. Fenton put a fresh clip in his Sten gun and readied himself for the charge. He threw himself under a bunk bed, sent out a burst of fire to greet the soldiers who charged into the area. Another group tried to enter through a window and he shot them dead.

They used tear gas. He ran after the first shell and threw it out at them, but the second one went off and filled the small wooden building with thick, eye-burning smoke. He knew better than to try to hold out against it. He broke open the Sten gun and fitted it with a full clip, his last. He left the musette bag behind and raced outside, his finger on the Sten gun's trigger.

He did not stop shooting. He was surrounded and bullets came at him from all angles, but Fenton stubbornly refused to go down. He fired a full clip at the soldiers before he slumped and died.

The soldiers searched the barracks. They couldn't believe that this one little man had been the only invader, but there was no one else around, no one but their own dead soldiers.

Someone took the trouble to count the bullets in Fenton. There were sixty-three of them. Machine gun slugs had almost torn him in half.

And, strangest of all, what was left of his face seemed to be smiling.

✦

Hines awoke early Sunday morning. The room was dark because sunlight never reached the basement. He switched on a light and glanced at his watch. It was not yet seven. He tried catching another hour's sleep but found it impossible. He got out of bed, washed, dressed.

At eight o'clock Señora Luchar brought him breakfast—oatmeal, fresh fruits, biscuits and coffee. She left him and he tried to eat. The food stuck in his throat. He could not possibly have been less hungry.

When she came down for the tray she saw that he had eaten nothing. "There is something wrong with the food?" she said. "You cannot eat it?"

"The food's fine. I'm not hungry."

"You are nervous?"

He said nothing because he did not know how to answer her. He was not nervous, not exactly. He wasn't sure how to describe the feelings he had. He looked at his watch. The time was crawling.

"You should eat. Today will be an important day. Murder is hard work and work is difficult on an empty stomach."

Hard work? All he had to do was toss a bomb in the air. But her words somehow intimidated him. He picked up his fork and ate some of his food. Then he drank the coffee.

"An important day," she went on. "And you are doing something for Cuba as well as for your brother, Hines. That, too, is important."

She left him, sparing him the need to answer her. Between then and noon he went four times to the work bench, and four times he picked up the bomb and hefted it in his hand. It was cylindrical, roughly the size and shape of a can of beer, although of course much heavier. Each time he replaced the bomb on the bench and went back to his bunk.

He no longer thought of giving it all up, of running to the Swiss consulate and asking for asylum. He was committed now, and he did not even think of backing down. At noon he left the house. It was not time yet—Castro's speech was scheduled to start at five, the hour of bull fights. Hines remembered the García Lorca poem, the one in which every other line was *a las cinco de la tarde*, at five in the afternoon. A chilling, sobering poem about a bullfighter gored to death in the ring—

But he couldn't stay around the house. He waved a hand at the Luchar woman, nodded at the old man rocking stonily on the porch. He headed for the Plaza of the Revolution where Castro would speak. Already people were gathering. He would have to arrive early to get a good position.

But how early? He found a Cuban man who spoke English, told him he wanted to see Castro speak, asked him how soon he would have to be there to get a good spot in the crowd.

The man looked at him. "You are a Yankee?"

"Yes."

"That is good, then," the Cuban said. "More Yankees

should hear Fidel speak. There would be less trouble if you Yankees listened to our Fidel."

The man told him three o'clock would be time enough. Hines thanked him and left the square. He walked to a small lunch counter next door to the Hotel Nacional and had a cup of coffee. On an impulse he bought a pack of cigarettes and tried to smoke one. He choked on it and put it out, leaving the pack on the counter.

He went back to the house, went downstairs to the basement. Señora Luchar brought him a fresh pot of coffee and a bottle of whiskey to spike it with. He mixed whiskey and coffee half and half and drank a great quantity of it. The whiskey did not seem to have any effect on him. He did not get at all high. But the whiskey did counteract the coffee, which made him sweaty and irritable when he had too much of it.

At two-thirty he put on a loose jacket and tucked the bomb into one pocket of it. He said goodbye to Señora Luchar and left the house. She told him she wished him good luck and he thanked her. The old man on the porch said *buena suerte* and Hines smiled at him.

He walked to the Plaza de la Revolution, acutely aware of the way the bomb bulged his pocket and waiting every minute for someone to notice, to tap him on the shoulder, to place him under arrest. No one bothered him. He made his way to the square where a thick crowd was already forming. He inched forward

in the crowd, securing a perfect vantage point not at
all far from the steps of the palace.

He was sweating. He was not sure whether it was
the coffee, the crowd or the heat that made him per-
spire, or whether his fear was causing it. But somehow
he was not really afraid. Fear ceased to have anything
to do with it any more, just as logic had flown the coop
not long ago. It was three o'clock. Castro would begin
his speech in two hours. And the steps where he would
stand were just a stone's throw away.

A stone's throw. Or a bomb's throw.

Turner sat in a café on La Calle de Trabajadores. His
hotel room had no television set and he wanted to see
Castro's speech. He drank bottled beer and watched
the screen of the café's set.

At four-thirty a movie ended and the channel began
coverage of the speech. Castro was not yet due to
arrive for an hour, but the television cameras began by
panning the crowd while the announcer killed time by
reading news bulletins in rapid Spanish.

Today, Turner thought. Today, while I sit here
drinking this beer in this café. Today.

Maybe he was making a mistake. Maybe he should
be with Hines. Maybe the kid was right to call him
chicken. Maybe he was copping out, turning yellow.

But what good could he do? One man could throw a
bomb as well as two. One man could blow up a dic-

tator as well as two. And one man could surely die as well as two.

To hell with it. He had his own life to live. And if Jim Hines had his own death to die, well, that was his own damned business. And not Turner's.

He sipped his beer and watched the screen.

At a quarter to five Garrison locked and bolted his door. He took out a small penknife and slashed his mattress open again, pulling the high-powered rifle free. His window shade was drawn. Garrison broke down the gun, cleaned it, loaded it with a single bullet. When you are paid high prices for murder, you do not need more than one bullet. Not with an expensive rifle fitted with a scope sight and zeroed in on a stationary target. One bullet was plenty.

He switched off the light in the room. That way there was much less chance of drawing attention from the street. Then he raised the shade a few inches and planted himself in a chair by the window. Castro hadn't arrived yet but the plaza was jammed already, filled with a noisy mass of people. It was odd, sitting above them all in solitary comfort, knowing something that they could not know. Like watching a movie when you knew the ending in advance. A special feeling, a combination of superiority and, somehow, disappointment.

At five minutes to five he got the rifle in position.

He propped a pillow on the windowsill, then rested the rifle upon it. The pillow would steady the gun, absorb a certain amount of the recoil, and muffle a certain amount of the noise. He knelt by the window and held tight to the rifle. He sighted in on the speaker's platform on the steps of the Palace of Justice.

Castro appeared at four minutes after the hour. His soldiers cleared a path for him through the crowd and the big bearded man walked up the path to the platform. He wore his usual uniform—army boots, a field jacket, khaki slacks, thick flowing beard. He stepped upon the platform and the applause thundered.

The applause did not stop. Garrison watched Castro, the man he had to kill. He watched him first over the rifle, then through the sight. The hairline cross in the scope was centered upon Castro's face, between his full mouth and his hawk-like nose. Garrison's finger touched the trigger, gently.

Not yet, he thought. Not for an hour, maybe. Because the less time he spent in Cuba after he squeezed that trigger, the safer it was. They could figure out where the bullet came from. They could run him down, meet him at the airport—

Something else was bothering him, he realized. It took him a while to figure out what it was.

He did not want to kill Castro.

Looking at his victim through the gunsight, seeing that hairline cross that marked the bullet's target, he knew suddenly that he did not want to kill this man.

This man was not like any of his other targets, and he couldn't expect to get away as easily afterwards. They might well catch him, here or at the airport, and if they caught him at the airport, they'd get Estrella, too.

He didn't want to think about what they would do to her.

Before, he might have risked it. Before, when it was just him. Now, he didn't want to.

But he had to—it was his job, wasn't it?

Not any more. He was quitting. The Cubans— Hiraldo and his boys—were not the syndicate. He could blow the job without worrying about any back-lash. They wouldn't kill him for it the way the outfit boys would.

But the money—he needed the dough, didn't he?

No, he thought. No, not really. He had maybe seven or eight grand set aside here and there throughout the States. With that much dough you could get set up nicely selling rifles and shotguns and shells in a medium-sized town. It wasn't a bad business and it was one he knew inside and out. Maybe pick up a few spare bucks giving shooting lessons or taking out hunting parties. And gunsmith work, gun repair. He knew the business and you didn't need more than what dough he already had to get started. And Estrella could help out in the store until they got going. And some-day his kids could come into the business with him.

He looked through the scope sight again. Castro was speaking now. He saw the muscles knotted in the thick neck, heard the booming voice. The crowd was silent now. Everyone listened to the man, to Fidel Castro. Everyone heard his voice and followed his words.

Estrella was going to be at the airport at seven. They would catch a plane to Miami. Then they could clear out the bank accounts, look for a shop. Maybe some medium-sized town in Washington, maybe Oregon. It was good country up there. His country, the country he had been born in.

But twenty grand—

He looked at Castro. Automatically his finger found the trigger, caressed it.

No.

No, because there was too much to lose now.

He brought the rifle back from its perch and returned it to its place in the slashed mattress. He put the sheets and blankets back on the bed and tucked them in. He returned the pillow from the windowsill to the bed, closed the window, drew the shade. Now to check out. Or, better yet, now to leave. If he checked out they might unmake the bed and find the gun. If he left he would be in Miami before a maid saw the inside of the room. They could keep his luggage as payment for the bill he would be skipping. All except the volume of Rimbaud. He got the book, slipped it into a pocket. He would have to try reading Rimbaud to Estrella. She might like the poems.

He was halfway to the door when the bomb went off.

The noise was tremendous. Garrison wheeled around, ran to the window. He raised the shade and stared out.

Castro was dead. That was the first thing he saw— Fidel Castro, his legs blown away, his blood flowing freely. Castro, sprawling legless across the nearly demolished speakers' platform. Other men, near him, screaming, wounded, dying.

Then Garrison looked for the bomber. The whole crowd was in a turmoil, women shrieking, children crying, men shouting. Police officers fired their guns into the air. A riot seemed imminent.

And then Garrison spotted the one who'd thrown the bomb. It was a kid, he saw, a young kid hardly old enough to shave. And then he recognized the kid. It was Hines, one of the four others from Hiraldo's confab in Tampa. Hines had done it—Hines had thrown the bomb and killed Castro.

Now Garrison stood watching Hines pay the penalty.

It was an awful penalty. The crowd mobbed the boy, grabbing at him, kicking at him. Garrison looked on in silence as the crowd beat Hines to death before his eyes. By the time the police forced their way through the crowd, Hines was dead. He lay on the ground. Broken, dead.

Garrison sat for a moment. He smoked a cigarette, ground it out in an ashtray. Then he left the room and the hotel.

The money was waiting for him in Miami. But he knew instinctively that it was money he would never touch. He had done nothing to earn it. Whatever fraction of the hundred thousand was his, he didn't need it. He would manage on what he had of his own.

He waded through the turmoil around the hotel, fought his way through the screaming, anguished crowd. Three blocks away, he found a taxi and told the driver to take him to the airport.

Would Estrella be there? Would she have heard the news and fled, to whatever dim corner of the city she called her home? Or would she loyally be waiting for him, nervousness showing in her eyes, attracting the attention of airport officials around her?

Were any flights even going to be permitted, or would all planes now be grounded, all would-be passengers scrutinized by armed police officers, subjected to interrogation at any sign of anxiety or hint of guilty knowledge?

The airport building loomed in the taxi windshield.

Garrison had never been nervous before, on any of his jobs. He'd killed many men, and his hands had never shaken, before or after. Now he'd done nothing, killed no one—but he felt his palms sweating.

Estrella would be there, he told himself.

She would be there, and he would take her away with him.

He opened the door.

THE
END

Get Hard Case Crime by Mail...
And Save 43%!

☐ **YES! Sign me up for the Hard Case Crime Book Club!**

As long as I choose to stay in the club, I will receive every Hard Case Crime book as it is published (generally one each month). I'll get to preview each title for 10 days. If I decide to keep it, I will pay only $3.99* — a savings of 43% off the cover price! There is no minimum number of books I must buy and I may cancel my membership at any time.

Name: _____

Address: _____

City / State / ZIP: _____

Telephone: _____

E-Mail: _____

☐ **I want to pay by credit card:** ☐ VISA ☐ MasterCard ☐ Discover

Card #: _____ Exp. date: _____

Signature: _____

Mail this page to:
HARD CASE CRIME BOOK CLUB
20 Academy Street, Norwalk, CT 06850-4032

Or fax it to 610-995-9274.
You can also sign up online at www.dorchesterpub.com.

* Plus $2.00 for shipping. Offer open to residents of the U.S. and Canada only. Canadian residents please call 1-800-481-9191 for pricing information.

If you are under 18, a parent or guardian must sign. Terms, prices, and conditions subject to change. Subscription subject to acceptance. Dorchester Publishing reserves the right to reject any order or cancel any subscription.

3 1170 00800 7852